My flight's being ca_____p.

"Mom, Dad," Elizabeth began. "I have something to tell you. Earlier this year I applied to a semester-abroad program. I've been accepted to the University of London for the fall. A semester away from Sweet Valley is exactly what I need. And I've decided to go." She raised her ticket so that they could see it. "And now my flight's being called."

"I don't care what you've decided," Mr. Wakefield said, hands on hips. "I'm your father, and I've decided that you're coming with us to see Jessica and settle things."

Her parents weren't even listening to her. All they seemed to care about was Jessica. Jessica, Jessica, Jessica.

Elizabeth slung her backpack over her shoulder and gripped her ticket. "I'm sorry. I'm sorry we have to part like this. But I'm going to London."

She turned around and squeezed shut her eyes, walking slowly toward the line of people waiting to board. She half expected her father to tackle her, her mom to drag her out to a waiting taxicab . . . but there was nothing, except the frantic screams they directed toward her.

"Elizabeth! Come back!" her mom cried.

But Elizabeth didn't. She took a deep breath, handed the ticket to the flight attendant, and boarded the plane.

Elizabeth

University

Wi
Lau

Cr
FRANC

NEW YORK · TORONTO · AUCKLAND

RL: 8, AGES 014 AND UP

UNIVERSITY, INTERRUPTED
A Bantam Book / January 2001

Produced by 17th Street Productions,
an Alloy Online, Inc. company.
33 West 17th Street
New York, NY 10011.

ISBN: 0-553-49353-1

Visit us on the Web! www.randomhouse.com/teens

Published simultaneously in the United States and Canada

Bantam Books is an imprint of Random House Children's Books, a division
of Random House, Inc. BANTAM BOOKS and the rooster colophon are
registered trademarks of Random House, Inc. Bantam Books, 1540
Broadway, New York, New York 10036.

PRINTED IN THE UNITED STATES OF AMERICA

OPM   0 9 8 7 6 5 4 3 2 1

To Hilary Bloom

Chapter One

Outside Chicago, Illinois

Nineteen-year-old Elizabeth Wakefield was weeks away from starting her junior year. And soon she'd be twenty. All grown up.

So why am I sitting in this all-night diner, afraid to get back in the Jeep and drive to the airport? she wondered. *And why does the thought of getting on a plane to London scare the stuffing out of me? After all, the University of London is waiting for me. I have the scholarship acceptance letter in my backpack to prove it.*

And why can't I stop crying?

Because London is a million miles away from Sweet Valley, from SVU, from your family—

Her family. *That was a joke,* Elizabeth thought, her stomach twisting.

1

Family *doesn't totally betray you out of the blue.* Family *doesn't pretend to hate your boyfriend and then hook up with him.* Family *doesn't—*

"Can I get you anything else, miss?"

Elizabeth glanced up at the waitress who'd been pouring her cups of bad coffee for the past three hours. Luckily the waitress didn't seem to mind that Elizabeth had been taking up a booth since six o'clock that morning. "Uh, no, thanks," Elizabeth told her, barely able to lift her head, let alone return the woman's cheerful expression. "I'm fine," she added with a pathetic attempt at a smile.

Elizabeth took a deep breath. *At least I managed to say three words without bursting into tears,* she told herself. *That's a major improvement.*

"You don't look fine," the waitress said, her warm smile replaced by a worried frown. "In fact, you look like you just lost your best friend."

Make that plural, Elizabeth thought, tears pooling in her eyes. *My boyfriend and my sister. I thought I had two best friends. Now I have none. Now I have no one.*

Elizabeth was grateful when the waitress was called away by another customer. One more kind word and she would have started sobbing into her chipped coffee cup.

For the millionth time since catching Jessica

2

Wakefield and Sam Burgess all over each other in the hallway of their motel last night, Elizabeth wondered why and how. *Why* Jessica had gone for Sam. Especially when she had her own boyfriend next door—a wonderful boyfriend who Jessica had professed to be in love with. But the real question was how: *how* Jessica, her own identical twin sister— the girl she'd spent practically every second with for the past nineteen years—could have done it, could have betrayed her. It made no sense.

For hours last night Elizabeth had racked her brain, the brain she was so famous for having, try- ing to figure out the answer to that very question: How.

Some people who knew the Wakefield twins would probably say: *Come on, Elizabeth. Jessica's like that. It doesn't mean anything. She can't help herself. Give her a break. You're the smart twin. . . .*

Yes, Elizabeth was the smart twin. Jessica was the flighty twin. Elizabeth was practical and re- sponsible. Jessica was superficial and impulsive. Elizabeth was into romance and love . . . Jessica was into as many cute guys as she could meet.

Elizabeth stared at her half-full coffee cup. Jessica was all those things, yes, but she'd also changed a lot during their sophomore year. She'd matured, gotten more serious about her schoolwork, about her friends, her sorority, her commitments. And she'd gotten less interested in hooking up with every hot guy she picked up at SVU and more interested in finding one guy she could fall in love with.

And then there was Elizabeth, who'd changed a lot herself. As Jessica had become more like Elizabeth, Elizabeth had become more like her sister. She'd decided to focus her studies on creative writing instead of journalism, for one. Facts and right answers suddenly weren't all that mattered, Elizabeth had discovered; life wasn't black and white. And so she'd started being less uptight. Less Little Ms. Perfect. Okay, she hadn't exactly cut classes or taken up lying as a hobby. But she'd been willing to open her eyes and look at life in different ways, instead of the "Elizabeth Wakefield" way.

And what she'd seen had just about killed her.

Her own sister with her boyfriend.

And so she was back to *how*. How could Jessica have done it?

Not that she wasn't angry with Sam. She couldn't even think about Sam without either tearing up or feeling like throwing her coffee cup clear across the diner. But Sam wasn't her blood. He wasn't her family. He wasn't her twin sister.

Elizabeth eyed the plates of scrambled eggs, greasy home fries, and bacon that the waitress was delivering to the next table. She couldn't imagine eating a bite ever again.

The waitress refilled Elizabeth's coffee cup as she passed by, and Elizabeth sent her a silent thank-you. If Elizabeth ever ended up around here again, if she ever just so happened to be somewhere outside Chicago, Illinois, again, she'd come back with a little gift for the waitress who'd been so kind to her.

But Elizabeth doubted she'd ever set foot in Illinois again. Or any of the states between here and Sweet Valley, California. The very states in which she, Jessica, Sam, and Jessica's new boyfriend, Tyler, had driven on their way cross-country.

Had it been just days ago that Jessica had bounded into their off-campus house on SVU's campus with her master plan for a couples' road trip? Elizabeth and Sam, who'd finally hooked up after a year of flirting and fighting, had decided to drive from California to Boston, where Sam had a family wedding to attend. Elizabeth had been so excited about a cross-country road trip with Sam, culminating in meeting his family. And when Jessica had mentioned that Tyler was desperate for a ride to Illinois (for his sister's high-school graduation), Sam had been thrilled to have someone helping with gas and tolls. And since Tyler was coming, Jessica was coming too. Sam hadn't been too pleased to hear that, mostly because he and Jessica had never gotten along very well. Plus Jessica had made it crystal clear that she thought Sam was totally beneath Elizabeth. But since it meant so much to Elizabeth for him and Jessica to get to know each other, to see how great the other was, he'd finally agreed.

Good going, Liz, she thought. *You definitely got your wish. Sam and Jessica sure got to see how great the other was.*

As the images from last night flooded her mind, Elizabeth squeezed her eyes shut and concentrated on massaging the small of her back, which was screaming in pain. She'd spent the night in the Jeep, none too comfortable and none too conducive to sleeping—especially since she'd parked in the back of the diner's lot and spent the night worrying that a serial killer would knock on the window at any second.

Like she could have slept anyway. She'd been too busy crying her eyes out.

Now all she wanted was to go home, crawl into her bed in her parents' house, and have her mother soothe her, tell her everything was going to be all right.

But she couldn't go home. Not to Sweet Valley. Not to where Sam would be. Where Jessica was. Where life would never be the same for Elizabeth again. Besides, it wasn't as if Elizabeth could tell her parents what happened. It wasn't that it was too painful or humiliating. It was that it was simply *unspeakable*. Was that because there were no words to describe how it felt to have your own twin sister go for the guy she knew you loved? Knew you were planning to give your virginity to? Knew you wanted to be with forever?

Yeah, she had a feeling it was because there were no words to describe the pain of that.

And she'd be a fool to think her mother could make everything okay again. Because nothing would ever be all right.

Stop it! she ordered herself. *You're not a kid. You're an adult. You're almost twenty years old! You can't go home. And you have a scholarship for the fall semester to the University of London in your backpack. Pay for your five cups of coffee, wash your hands and face, and get back in that Jeep. Drive to the airport. And get on a plane to London.*

It's that simple.

Elizabeth jumped up, then sat right back down.

It wasn't that simple. Gnawing her lower lip, Elizabeth signaled the waitress for another refill.

A half hour later, Elizabeth ordered a stack of pancakes that she didn't plan to eat, just so she wouldn't feel so guilty taking up the table in the diner. While she waited for her food, Elizabeth made a trip to the Jeep.

The warm, sunny May morning was so cheerful, but it did nothing to help Elizabeth's state of mind. She unlocked the Jeep and lugged her duffel onto the front seat. She pulled out her cosmetics case, a pair of underwear, a white T-shirt, and her pale blue cardigan sweater, then stuffed the duffel back under the seat. She'd packed for a two-week summer cross-country road trip. That meant she had only the basics; well, except for the fancy black sleeveless dress and high-heeled sandals she'd brought for the wedding she'd thought she'd be attending with Sam. She had two pairs of shorts, her favorite jeans, a few T-shirts, two thin cardigans, one cotton slip dress, and a few bathing suits. That would get her through the fall semester in London, wouldn't it?

Yeah, if London weren't cold and rainy and London, she reminded herself. *London's a major city. You can't dress for the beach!*

Well, you're not there yet. Worry about it when you get there. Besides, you have a credit card. You can always buy some decent basics when you get there and see what everyone else wears.

For now she'd wash her face, brush her teeth, put eyedrops in her puffy blue-green eyes, tie her long, blond hair in a high ponytail, change her underwear and her wrinkly shirt, and maybe feel like a person again. Then maybe she'd get up the guts to drive to the airport.

Five minutes later she sat back down at her table, the plate of fresh, hot pancakes waiting for her. Maybe it was the fresh air or a clean face, but suddenly Elizabeth was starving. She dug into the pancakes with one hand and poured a mound of maple syrup with the other.

Sam loved maple syrup on his pancakes.

And if Jessica were here, she'd have made Mickey Mouse ears out of the pancakes . . .

Suddenly in her mind's eye Elizabeth saw Jessica and Sam making out in the hallway of the motel as if they were standing in the diner. Sam's mouth crushing Jessica's . . . Jessica's hands all over Sam's chest . . .

The fork dropped out of Elizabeth's hand and clattered to the floor.

"I'll grab you another fork if I can share your table."

Elizabeth glanced up to see a pretty girl with long, straight brown hair, wearing jeans and a tie-dyed T-shirt, grinning at her. The girl picked up the fork and dropped it in a bin of dirty plates.

"Every table is taken, so if you're alone, is it okay if I sit here?" she asked. She snatched a fork from the waitress station and handed it to Elizabeth with a smile.

"Uh, thanks, and yeah, sure, you can sit here."

"Cool!" the girl said, her brown eyes twinkling. She plopped down, then buried her freckled nose in the menu.

Elizabeth tried to blink back the tears that had pooled in her eyes at the image of her sister and Sam. *Stop thinking about them!* she ordered herself. She took a deep breath. *Think about something else. Like the front of the girl's menu. Your coffee cup. The chandeliers hanging from the ceiling. The fly-specked posters decorating the dreary walls of the coffee shop.* Elizabeth's gaze drifted over faded pictures of coral reefs and the Eiffel Tower until coming to rest on a lopsided picture of Buckingham Palace. Elizabeth blinked twice and stared hard at the poster of the famous London monument.

It's an omen, she thought. *It has to be.*

She grabbed her backpack and dug through it with renewed energy. Her wallet, the keys to the Jeep, and a tube of Chap Stick tumbled out onto her lap. She rifled through the pack until her hand closed on a long, white envelope. She stuffed everything else back inside, then pushed aside her pancakes and laid the envelope on the table. Her fingers trembled as she withdrew the letter contained inside.

We wish to inform you that you have been

accepted to attend, on full scholarship, the fall semester at the University of London . . . as a visiting creative-writing fellow. . . .

Elizabeth had received the letter of acceptance not long ago. She'd applied for the prestigious creative-writing program back when she and Sam had been fighting this past winter, back when she'd thought they'd never get together. Back then, a semester away from Sam—an ocean away from Sam—had seemed exactly what she needed. But she and Sam had hooked up at last, just before finals. And the thought of leaving him and their fragile relationship, even for a semester, had been unbearable. She'd wanted to make up her own mind, so she hadn't told anyone she'd applied or been accepted. But Jessica being Jessica had, of course, snooped through Elizabeth's things and had found the letter. She'd been pushing Elizabeth to go. Insisted it was an opportunity Elizabeth couldn't pass up for some guy. That she'd be crazy not to accept the scholarship.

So she could have Sam for herself? Elizabeth wondered.

Elizabeth had put the University of London out of her mind. All she'd wanted to concentrate on for the summer was Sam. And now the summer had hardly begun, and here Elizabeth was. Alone in a diner in the middle of the country, sitting across a table from a total stranger studying her menu.

"How's the coffee here?" asked the girl as she put down the menu. She leaned back against the seat and smiled at Elizabeth. "My name's Daphne, by the way."

"I'm Elizabeth, and it's not that bad once you add about a cup of cream and sugar."

Daphne nodded. The waitress came over and took her order. "So do you go to school around here? I just graduated from the University of Chicago. Sociology major."

"Wow, that's a great school," Elizabeth said. It felt good to talk to someone else, good to think about something other than herself. She listened as Daphne rattled off all the things she'd had to do over the past few weeks—turning in her final papers, taking exams, packing up her apartment, saying good-bye to her friends who were scattering across the country.

"I'll miss everybody, but I am just so psyched I'm done!" Daphne exclaimed as the waitress delivered her coffee. "I'm on my way to the airport but figured I'd stop here for some chow since airport prices are, like, astronomical."

"Where are you headed?" Elizabeth asked, cutting a bite of pancake.

"I'm meeting up with my boyfriend in London." Daphne paused as the waitress set a plate of bacon and scrambled eggs down in front of her. "We're going to hang out there for a few weeks and then head over to France and bum around Europe for a while. I think I'll probably take about six months off, maybe the whole year, before I come back and do the career thing." She poured some cream and sugar into her coffee and then took a swig. "You weren't kidding," she said with a grimace. "What'd they put in this stuff? Battery acid?" She dumped some more sugar in.

"A whole *year?*" Elizabeth's jaw dropped in amazement. She couldn't imagine aimlessly wandering across Europe, with no goal in mind other than whatever seemed interesting. What would it be like to be that free?

Look at me, she thought ruefully. *Even though my life in Sweet Valley is over, even though I have a scholarship waiting for me in London, I can't even make myself go to the* airport, *let alone fly off to a foreign country. And look at her. No scholarship, no plans, and she's all ready to do her own thing, her own way. No rules, no goals, no nothing except her own ideas.*

"So you're okay with putting off finding a job for a whole year?" Elizabeth asked. "Aren't you at all stressed about what will happen when you get back? What do your parents have to say about it?"

Daphne shrugged as she attacked the plate of scrambled eggs. "Well, first of all, I'm twenty-two, so even if they wanted to, there's not a whole lot that they could say. I mean, I love them, but I've got to live my own life, right?"

13

Elizabeth nodded. She had barely even considered her parents' reaction to her going to London. How would they feel if she suddenly called them to say she was leaving the country for the semester to live alone in London? They'd flip. Wouldn't they?

But the reality was, Elizabeth was an adult. A responsible adult. If she wanted to go abroad for the fall semester of her junior year, she was well within her rights to. Plus hadn't she won the scholarship?

So why am I so worried about what Mom and Dad will say? she wondered. *Why am I such a scaredy-cat?*

"But the truth is, they're pretty cool about it," Daphne continued, shaking some ketchup onto her eggs.

Elizabeth looked away. Sam was the only other person she knew who liked ketchup on his eggs. And any reminder of Sam was enough to make her start crying again.

"You okay?" Daphne asked. "You look a little green."

Elizabeth managed to smile. "I'm okay." And she would be. As long as she didn't look at Daphne's eggs or the radio didn't start playing one of her and Sam's favorite songs. Or she didn't catch a glimpse of a guy with sandy blond hair and hazel eyes and an amazing body.

"So your parents are really okay with your plans?" she asked, curious.

14

Daphne smiled. "They know that I'm focused. I was a good student; I've been responsible; they know they can trust me. Considering that I'll be working for the next, what, forty years? I think I deserve a year at this age to bum around and see the world."

Elizabeth nodded thoughtfully. "I guess you have a point." She forked a piece of pancake and dunked it in syrup. "I never thought about it that way before. I mean, you're totally right about working for the next hundred years. Plus other responsibilities come into play, like getting married, having kids. If you're ever going to go to Europe, now's the time."

She gnawed her lower lip and pushed around the last of the pancakes on her plate. Daphne made it all look so easy. Could it really be that easy for her too? Could she really just get up, drive to the airport, and go halfway around the world?

"Hey, I better get moving," Daphne exclaimed, looking at her watch. "I'm supposed to catch the airport shuttle in twenty minutes, and the stop's ten blocks away."

"Don't worry," Elizabeth said suddenly, a wave of determination swelling up inside her. "I'll drive you." She reached into her bag and closed her hand around the keys to the Jeep. "I'm going to O'Hare myself, in fact." Elizabeth signaled the waitress for the check and began gathering her things. "I'm going to London too."

Chapter
Two

Jessica Wakefield stared at her boyfriend, begging him with her eyes.

Her *ex*-boyfriend, unless she could somehow, some way make him understand.

"Please, Tyler, you have to listen to me," Jessica pleaded.

The air inside their tiny Illinois motel room was stifling. The brown carpet was stained, the picture on the small TV barely came in, and there was a persistent *drip, drip, drip* in the old porcelain sink that was driving Jessica crazy. She tried to block out the eyesore they were in and concentrate on what mattered: getting Tyler to listen to her and realize what she was saying was the truth.

It wasn't going to be easy.

Tyler leaned his lanky frame in the high-backed wooden chair by the window, his long legs sprawled in front of him. Sunlight splayed through the flimsy curtain, splashing against his broad, T-shirt-clad shoulders. His normally sweet lips had curled into a skeptical sneer.

Jessica sat fidgeting with the hem of her shorts on the edge of the lumpy motel bed and tried to take small, even breaths. Tyler was so wonderful—gorgeous, sweet, smart, funny, and warm. She couldn't let him break up with her. Tears stung the backs of her eyes.

Even though they hadn't done more than kiss and cuddle since they'd left Sweet Valley days before, Jessica felt closer to Tyler than anyone she'd ever met. That was how in sync they'd been. How in love they'd been.

And now . . .

Jessica had pleaded with Tyler from the moment Elizabeth had screamed at her and sped away in the Jeep last night. He'd stormed out before Elizabeth had, but had come back, demanding an explanation. Jessica had pleaded with him to understand, to listen. But he'd been too upset to hear her. They'd passed out from exhaustion around two in the morning. And when Tyler had woken up an hour ago, he'd grabbed his duffel and was storming out of their room toward the parking lot when Jessica had convinced him to come back inside and listen. He'd finally, reluctantly, agreed.

17

Jessica was surprised Tyler had stayed to listen this long. *Because he really did love you*, she thought. *He loved you, and you threw it away. He's still here because he's hoping, praying, you'll say something that'll make what happened last night seem like a bad dream that never really happened.*

But it *had* happened.

"Okay, Tyler," she began. "The only thing I can do is swear on my life that everything I'm going to tell you is the absolute truth."

Tyler raised an eyebrow and stared at her. "Go ahead. I'm listening."

Jessica took a deep breath. "I'm going to start at the beginning again, okay?"

He nodded.

"You know how I caught Sam making out with that girl yesterday, right?" Tyler nodded again. "And you also know that I told Elizabeth, but she wouldn't believe me. She thought I hated Sam so much, I'd do anything to break them up."

Tyler stood up. "Jessica, I'm waiting for you to tell me something I don't already know."

"Please," Jessica said. "I'm getting there. Really."

Tyler sighed and dropped back down on the chair.

"Elizabeth told me she was ready to sleep with Sam," Jessica said.

"So you told me," Tyler commented impatiently.

18

Jessica stared at him. "*So* I couldn't let her do it. I couldn't let her lose her virginity to that two-timing jerk!" She stood up and began pacing the tiny room. She felt like her whole future depended on Tyler understanding exactly what had *really* happened the night before. It was difficult to defend herself, though, when each time she glanced his way, his handsome face was stony.

"Yeah, I know how freaked you were about Elizabeth sleeping with Sam," Tyler said. "And I told you what I thought about that—it's none of your business."

"Tyler, you don't understand how *serious* Elizabeth is," Jessica explained, sitting back down on the bed. "She's managed to stay a virgin through two very serious boyfriends and a lot of pressure from a med student she recently fell for. She wouldn't sleep with a guy unless she believed they were forever."

"Jessica, that's still *her* business. Not yours."

"We're twins, Tyler. Identical twins. Elizabeth isn't just my sister. We're closer than anyone can imagine."

"Okay, fine." Tyler's voice was cold. "So you're way overprotective, whatever. That's not the issue here. Get to the point. I'm giving you five minutes, Jessica. Then I'm out of here."

"I thought that if I showed Elizabeth what a

pig Sam really was, then she wouldn't sleep with him," Jessica told Tyler for the tenth time since last night. "I thought if she saw me and Sam making out, she'd kick him to the curb."

Tyler let out a mean, sharp laugh. "So you broke up Sam and Elizabeth, just like you wanted, but it was you who got kicked to the curb, Jess."

Jessica shook her head. "You're not getting it. Sam makes me sick! There was no way I could sit back and let her make that kind of mistake . . . something she could never undo! Don't you understand? I had to break them up! I planned and plotted the whole thing, Tyler. That's what I've been trying to tell you for hours now."

Tyler yawned. "Anything else?"

Jessica fought the urge to rush to him and beg him to stay with her. She *could* do this. She was telling the truth, from her heart. He had to listen. "So last night I decided to fool Sam into thinking I was Elizabeth, then come on to him where we would definitely be seen by her." Jessica shuddered as she remembered the feel of Sam's hands wandering all over her body. She shook her head in disgust and rubbed her hands down the sides of her shirt as if she could wipe away his touch. "It worked. He believed I was Elizabeth. And when Elizabeth saw us, she freaked."

The plan had worked. Too well, though. Because

Jessica hadn't considered one very important fact when she'd gone ahead with her supposedly brilliant plot to break up Sam and Elizabeth . . . she had forgotten that Elizabeth wouldn't be calm enough to understand any of Jessica's reasons. She'd only feel betrayed.

Jessica would never forget the look on her sister's face when she'd told Jessica they were no longer sisters and had then slammed out of the room. Jessica had run after Elizabeth, but Elizabeth had sped away in the Jeep and tore off into the middle of the night. And Sam? Sam had taken off just as fast.

"Oh, I get it now," Tyler said, nodding slowly. "I understand."

"You do?" Jessica felt the first stirrings of hope.

"Yeah, sure," Tyler said coldly. "You think you're God."

"Whaaa?" Jessica gaped. "I thought you said you understood!"

"Do everyone in your life a favor and grow up, Jess," he said as he grabbed his duffel and flung open the door. "You're a little too old to act before you think. You didn't give two figs for how I'd feel, how your sister would feel, or how Sam would feel. You just took matters into your own hands and hurt everyone involved." Tyler clomped down the hall and down the outdoor stairwell.

"Tyler!" Jessica raced down the stairs after him, her sandals banging noisily on the cement. She was dimly aware that an older couple unlocking their door and a maid pushing a cleaning cart were staring at them, but she didn't care. She had to get through to Tyler. She had to make him understand. For Elizabeth's sake, she'd had to make some sacrifices. She'd had no choice. *No choice*. Why couldn't he understand that?

She followed him through the parking lot onto the dusty road, alternately babbling and crying. Nothing worked. Ignoring her, he walked over to the edge of the one-lane highway with his thumb extended.

"Tyler, come on," she begged, grabbing his arm.

He shook her off as if she were a bug. "Look, Jess. I'm just not into these head games. If you want to manipulate your sister's love life, go ahead. But I'm not going to stick around and watch. I've got to get home for my sister's graduation."

Hurt and frustration swirled in her empty stomach as she stood there, inches away from Tyler, watching him as he squinted out into the sunlight. She'd been an idiot to think that he'd understand . . . that he'd applaud her efforts to save her sister from a creep. In the end, all that Tyler would remember was Jessica's lips as they pressed against Sam's.

When a gas truck rumbled to a stop alongside them, Tyler climbed inside without a backward glance. All Jessica's hopes disappeared in a cloud of dust as the truck roared off down the highway.

Now what? Jessica stared at the back of the truck until it was no more than a speck on the horizon. Jessica couldn't remember ever feeling this helpless and forlorn in her life. Her sister hated her, the guy she loved despised her, and she was stranded in some town in the middle of nowhere in the middle of the country without ten bucks to her name. What the heck was she going to do? She didn't know where to go or what she would do when she got there, but it didn't really matter because she didn't have the energy to move anyway. Half of her was tempted to just give up and lie down by the side of the road.

Jessica sighed and turned back toward the motel. She'd have to figure out something. The question was, what? Maybe she could hitch a ride with someone too. *Yeah, right,* she thought. *Like hitchhiking is really safe.*

So what do I do? she wondered as she kicked a stone out of her path. *I've got no money and no way out of here. And suppose by some miracle I make it back to Sweet Valley. Then what? If I try to tell Elizabeth the truth about what I did, she'll never believe me. And if she does, she'll just go right back to*

Sam and beg him for forgiveness! Jessica realized, her heart breaking completely.

She gnawed her lower lip as she walked up the steps to the motel and pushed through the peeling double doors. Her stomach was grumbling and twisting at the same time. She could forget eating breakfast even if she could manage to swallow a bite of toast. She had about seven dollars, and she'd need it for bus fare to Chicago, where she could catch a plane home.

"So will that be cash or credit?"

Jessica glanced at the clerk behind the reception desk. The middle-aged man was staring at Jessica with a strained smile.

Oops. Jessica felt her stomach drop to her toes. Her seven bucks wouldn't quite cover the bill for the rooms, and Jessica's credit card was totally maxed out.

Jessica tried to flash him one of her most dazzling smiles, but her heart wasn't in it, and she knew that it came out crooked.

He handed her a long, pink piece of paper: the motel bill for both rooms. "You seem to be the only person in your party who is still on the premises, and checkout time was a half hour ago. Cash or credit card, miss?"

Jessica eyed the pink bill. "You can't be serious!" She gasped in amazement as she stared at the paper that the clerk had thrust under her nose. "There's no way I can owe that much!" She scanned it frantically, hoping there was some mistake.

How could it be so expensive? Jessica wondered angrily. After all, it wasn't as if they were staying at the Ritz! She pressed a hand to her forehead as she studied the bill again, the pain in her head starting to compete with the gnawing in her stomach. *I know why it's so expensive!* She groaned. It wasn't that the rooms cost that much—if you split them *four* ways, but three of the four had cut out, leaving Jessica stuck with the bill.

"Which credit card will you be using today?" the clerk asked with a smile. Was it Jessica's imagination, or did he seem a shade less friendly than he had a few moments ago?

"Which credit card?" Jessica bit her lip and acted like she was considering one out of the hundreds that she might have while she thought frantically. "Um, here," she said, pulling out her silver Visa and pushing it across the counter.

She twisted her hair as he ran it through the machine and waited for the approval. She'd maxed out her Visa weeks ago, but maybe . . .

When he handed the card back to her a moment later, she couldn't say she was surprised.

"It's not taking this. Do you have another card you can put it on?" he asked, frowning.

"Try this one," Jessica suggested casually, handing him her MasterCard. She was so far behind in her payments, she was surprised she hadn't been thrown into debtors' prison, but would his little credit-card machine in this sorry excuse for a town *really* be able to know every detail about her credit history? She studied the clerk under her lashes as she chewed nervously at her lower lip.

"Sorry. This one's not going through either," he said after running it through the machine four times. He scratched his chin. "Any other ones you want to give a shot?"

If only he were cute, Jessica thought, taking in the man's beer belly, receding hairline, and hairy nostrils. At least then she'd be able to give an Academy Award–winning performance. No, that wasn't true. It wouldn't matter if he looked like Brad Pitt; as far as she was concerned, she never wanted to flirt again.

Well, here goes nothing, Jessica thought with a silent sigh as she glanced at the name tag pinned to his shirt. "So, Larry—" She smiled seductively and attempted to smooth her tangled hair. "I really want to give you another credit card. . . ." She paused, confident that the look she was giving him would drive all thought of cash or credit out of his mind.

"Okay, great." Larry tapped the credit-card

reader with a newsprint-stained finger. "Which one?"

Um, wrong response, Jessica thought, biting her lip in irritation. With most guys all it took was a sideways glance or a quirk of the eyebrow to have them gasping at her feet. What was wrong with this guy? Was he made of stone?

It's me who's made of stone, Jessica realized. As much as she wanted to get out of paying her bill, she couldn't summon the energy to move into flirting mode. Not only that, but her opening line had been extra weak.

Her shoulders slumped forward as she gave up all pretense of trying to charm him. "Look, Larry," Jessica said wearily. "I don't have any more credit cards, and I just don't have the bucks, okay? But can't we work something out here?"

"Work something out?" Larry's oily face was stern. "We have three methods of payment at the Moonbeam Motel. Credit cards, cash, and checks from people we know. There are no exceptions. Now, you say you don't have any credit cards or cash, and I sure don't know you. So any great ideas?"

Jessica could only offer a halfhearted, miserable shrug. Of course she didn't have a great idea. She didn't have *any* ideas. If she weren't so unhappy, she could probably think of something, but given the fact that her heart was breaking, she was amazed that she could even string two words together.

Well, I don't have the money to pay, Jessica thought, frowning as she considered her options. *Flirting sure didn't work—I guess that leaves only one thing.* Jessica sighed in despair. "Do you have a phone?" she asked dully. "I need to make a call."

"Right over there." Larry pointed to a phone booth in the corner.

Jessica plodded over to the phone booth as if her feet were dipped in cement. She opened the door and slumped down on the seat. *Now what?* She stared at the phone as if it might bite her. Just who was she going to call who might bail her out of this mess?

"I'm going to have to call Mom and Dad," she muttered unhappily. She shivered as she imagined telling them exactly *why* it was that she'd ended up all alone without her sister, their Jeep, or any money.

I'd rather face a firing squad! Jessica thought with a moan as she rested her head against the cool glass of the door. She looked toward the reception desk to see what Larry was up to.

Elizabeth!

Jessica nearly jumped for joy as a flash of blond ponytail caught her eye. Elizabeth was standing at the reception desk, talking to Larry.

Jessica didn't know whether to laugh or cry. She was so relieved. She should have known that Elizabeth would forgive her and focus her anger and hurt on Sam. She should have known her sister wouldn't leave her stranded and alone. Her sister, her *twin,* would have to be missing her too. There was no way that she and Elizabeth could stand to be permanently parted. Oh, sure, Elizabeth would still be furious. Jessica had no doubt that she'd be hearing all about it for the next hundred miles—*Well, probably more like all the way back to Sweet Valley,* Jessica figured. She wasn't quite sure how she was going to be able to make it up to Elizabeth, but she was sure grateful that she had the opportunity.

She pushed open the door and bounded to her feet with renewed energy.

"Elizabeth!" Jessica cried as she lunged toward the desk. "I've been so—" She stopped dead in her tracks as the girl at the desk turned around.

She wasn't Elizabeth. She was just a blond girl who happened to be wearing her hair in a ponytail. That was all.

Jessica swallowed the lump in her throat as she stared at the other girl. Would she go through the rest of her life chasing after girls with blond pony-tails and hoping that they were her sister?

"You make that phone call yet?" Larry asked. He looked irritated at being interrupted.

29

"I, uh, no. I'll make it now," Jessica said dispiritedly. She slunk back to the phone booth.

And I thought I was miserable before, Jessica thought, hanging her head as tears prickled behind her eyelids. She'd thought that she couldn't feel worse than she already did, but somehow having her hopes raised and then dashed like that had made her sink even lower.

She missed Elizabeth more than she would have thought possible. It was worse than breaking up with a boyfriend. It was worse than breaking up with a friend. It was worse than breaking up with a *sister*. She had lost her twin.

Jessica couldn't stop thinking about all the things that bound her to Elizabeth. She remembered the countless times Elizabeth had helped to cheer her up after she'd broken up with a guy. She remembered all the times she'd borrowed Elizabeth's clothes—and then returned them—stained. Elizabeth would shake her head, but she'd never really get mad.

Jessica remembered all the things they'd done together over the years, the petty arguments, the laughter, and the total inseparable closeness. Then she remembered that they were all gone—maybe forever.

Jessica eyed Larry. He was watching her. *Who the hell am I supposed to call?* she asked herself. *I'm in the middle of nowhere!*

Chapter Three

Elizabeth stood in line at O'Hare International Airport's British Airways ticket line, feeling more apprehensive by the minute. In contrast, Daphne was next to her, reading a guidebook on London without a care in the world.

I'll never be like Daphne, she thought miserably. *Why am I so uptight? Why am I so scared of the unknown? Do I have to have every single aspect of my life mapped out in order to exist peacefully?*

Yup. I do. Elizabeth crossed her arms over her chest and shivered in the air-conditioned airport. She'd been smart to wear her sweater, but even with it, she was freezing.

"Isn't this place wild?" Daphne exclaimed with a huge smile. "This airport is gigantic! But wait till you see Heathrow in England! This will be my second time there. I love it."

Elizabeth swallowed around the lump in her throat. It had taken her so long to figure out how to get from the arts building to the science center on SVU's campus. How was she supposed to navigate her way around a foreign airport, let alone a foreign country?

Elizabeth had been to the major international airport in Los Angeles, but southern California was completely familiar to her. Chicago, and this enormous terminal, seemed like another world. People were rushing all over the place, and there were so many different places to rush off to! Gates and destinations and security lines. Restaurants and fast-food courts. Miles of luxury shops and bookstores and magazine stands. And the air was filled with the chatter of thousands of people speaking every possible known language. Elizabeth had no problem recognizing French and Spanish. But what was that dark-haired, romantic-looking girl speaking? Was it Russian? Elizabeth tried to imagine what she was saying to her cute boyfriend, who looked a little bit like Sam. She swallowed hard again and looked away, afraid that she might start crying.

I have to keep focused on why I'm here, she told herself. *Don't get sidetracked or intimidated by how overwhelming everything is.*

Not that Elizabeth was going to buy her ticket

just yet. She wanted to sit down and figure out exactly what her financial situation was before plunking down her money. Besides, she'd never buy a ticket without comparing prices with other airlines.

Yeah, right, Elizabeth chided herself. *You're here on line with Daphne. You could buy a ticket when it's your turn at the counter. You're still scared. Still acting like a baby.*

Elizabeth craned her head and looked down the vast hallway toward the domestic departures. How easy it would be to head off in that direction instead! She'd get on a plane to Sweet Valley and be home in a couple of hours. Maybe going to London would be too much of a shock after all she'd been through. So she couldn't bear to live with Jessica again; did that mean she had to flee the country like an escaped criminal? Maybe she could move in with her good friend Nina Harper and start her junior year at SVU, just as she'd always planned.

It's a big campus; maybe I can avoid Jessica, Elizabeth thought hopefully. *And Sam goes to Orange County College. I'd never have to see him again.*

But how could she ever go back to SVU when Jessica and Sam and her old life were so tied up there?

"Great! My turn, finally," Daphne said, rushing up to a ticket agent. A few minutes later Daphne waved Elizabeth over. "I'm all set," she said, grasping a red-and-blue ticket tightly in her hand. "Your turn."

Elizabeth approached the counter. "I'd like a one-way ticket to London," she said, her heart pounding. "London, England," she clarified hastily.

The woman smiled. "There's only one," she said pleasantly, typing some numbers into her computer. "When did you wish to travel?"

"Today," Elizabeth blurted out. "As soon as possible."

The woman nodded and kept typing. "All right, then. I have several seats left on a flight that leaves this afternoon for eleven hundred ninety-nine dollars."

Elizabeth stared in disbelief at the woman behind the British Airways ticket counter. She couldn't have heard her correctly. There was no way a ticket could cost *that* much.

"I'm sorry," she said to the ticket agent, struggling to calm her voice. "I must have misheard you. *How* much is a one-way ticket to London?"

The agent smiled pleasantly. "Eleven hundred ninety-nine dollars—for same-day travel."

"But that's impossible!" Elizabeth cried. She was uncomfortably aware that the people behind her in line were starting to get restless, but for once she didn't care about making a scene. "I meant coach, not first class."

34

"First class?" The woman quirked an eyebrow and looked at Elizabeth like she was a child. "Hon, that is the coach fare."

"I don't understand," Elizabeth persisted in dismay. "What about those great fares I always see advertised to Paris and London? You know, round-trip tickets for three hundred bucks?"

Pleasant strained smile again. "That's when you buy a ticket six weeks in advance—not six hours. This is the best I—or any of the other airlines—can do for same-day travel. Do you want to purchase the ticket?"

"Well, yes, but not at that price," Elizabeth mumbled. She had only twelve hundred dollars' worth of credit on her Visa card. The fare would leave with her a buck!

"Hey, miss—" The man in line behind her thrust his head forward. "Do you mind hurrying up here? Some of us have planes to catch." He looked at her in irritation.

"Sorry," Elizabeth said. She hoisted her backpack on her shoulder and walked disconsolately away from the ticket desk to join Daphne, who was staring up at the departure screen on a TV above her head.

Forking over her credit card for an astronomical airfare just because she wanted to go to London was something Jessica would do. It would be totally irresponsible and impractical.

So what was *she* supposed to do?

"When's your flight?" Daphne asked.

Elizabeth was too embarrassed to tell her the truth. "Well, I—I want to wait a little longer before buying my ticket," she said, wondering if she'd ever be able to do it. "I wanted to check out some other airlines. Comparison shop."

Daphne shrugged. "Oh. Okay. So, how about you come with me to check my e-mail and we'll grab something to drink?"

Elizabeth nodded. *How could I spend so much money on an airline ticket?* she asked herself as they walked. If she bought the ticket to England, she'd have only a dollar left on her credit card. And she had only twenty-seven dollars in cash. Elizabeth mentally kicked herself for leaving her ATM card home; she'd done that on purpose so that she wouldn't go wild on the road trip. So much for being responsible! Now that she needed access to her checking account, she didn't have it. Then again, there wasn't much in it anyway. She'd known that until her student loan for the fall semester was posted to her account, she'd have to conserve as much cash as possible. So how had she managed to spend almost sixty dollars already?

It was possible that she'd counted wrong. After all, she was hardly thinking clearly. Not only had the events of the past twenty-four hours totally fried her brain, but she could barely concentrate with all the activity around her.

It wasn't just all the commotion of people rushing to catch their planes or the noise of the loud-speakers as they announced which flights were arriving. It was all the families and lovers saying good-bye that were playing havoc with Elizabeth's heart and mind.

It seemed like every time she turned around, she was face-to-face with sisters or couples or relatives or friends kissing and crying. Elizabeth forced herself to look away from a couple who were standing in her direct line of vision. *Where* had the money gone?

Of course. Elizabeth groaned. How could she have forgotten? Last night she'd spent a fortune buying bubble bath, scented candles, and *condoms!* She'd been so sure that she and Sam were finally going to make love. Her heart constricted in her chest as she recalled how excited and hopeful she'd been. Of course, that was before she realized that Sam and Jessica had plans of their own for the night.

How could she have been so blind? Ever since she and Sam had finally become a couple just weeks ago, she'd been closer and closer to feeling ready to sleep with him. Finally she *knew.* Felt in her heart that he was the one. But when she'd told

Sam that she was ready, finally ready, he'd been strangely reluctant to take her virginity. Jessica had been sure that was a bad sign, that Sam was saying they had all the time in the world because he couldn't deal with being Elizabeth's first. That it implied too much commitment for him.

At first Elizabeth had put a positive spin on their reactions. Sam didn't want to sleep with her because he did want Elizabeth to make sure she was ready, and Jessica, well, Jessica was just being hyperprotective. *Ha. Get a clue, Elizabeth.* Now, of course, she understood the real reason: They'd both tried to dissuade her because they only had eyes for each other.

Elizabeth choked back a sob as she followed Daphne through the busy terminal. It didn't matter how expensive it was to get to England. All that mattered was getting as far away from Jessica and Sam as humanly possible.

She had no doubt that the University of London would fix her up with a work-study program. Not only that, but as a visiting scholar, she'd be given a stipend, and her room and board would be taken care of by the scholarship.

Still . . .

Elizabeth couldn't deny that she was just plain scared at the thought of showing up in London with so little. What if something went wrong?

Deep in her heart she knew that everything would be fine, but the idea of being so broke made her feel vulnerable.

"Are you sure there's a place to hook up to the Internet here?" she asked Daphne as she followed her through the maze of people.

"Are you kidding?" Daphne said. "This is one of the biggest airports in the country. They've got this cybercafé called Laptop Land. Let's head over there."

Elizabeth and Daphne wended their way through the crowds toward a moving walkway. "This thing is weird," Elizabeth exclaimed as she stepped on it. "It's like a conveyor belt or something. Can't people get around under their own steam?"

"It is a little odd," Daphne agreed as she leaned against the railing. "It's great when you have really heavy bags, though."

Elizabeth nodded. She wished she had her own heavy bag. Maybe she'd feel more comfortable moving to London if she had more of her stuff. If she had known she'd be flying to London for a semester, she would have packed her wool sweaters and good pants, her raincoat, her leather walking boots, her books . . . gone shopping for new clothes and school supplies. All she had besides her duffel of summer clothes was a tattered copy of Jane Austen's *Pride and Prejudice*.

A crowd behind her surged onto the walkway, and Elizabeth was almost knocked over by a man pushing about ten suitcases in front of him. She was glad that Daphne seemed to know her way around because she had a bad feeling that she'd be lost without her. *How would I be able to handle London if I can't even handle O'Hare?* Elizabeth wondered anxiously. She noticed a woman hurrying by with a Venice Beach sticker on her suitcase and felt a wave of homesickness.

"There it is," Daphne said as they hopped off the ramp and walked into the enormous room known as Laptop Land. There must have been a thousand computer stations set up. They picked up a couple of coffees, then headed over to the nearest free station.

Elizabeth slid her backpack off on a stool and watched as Daphne logged on.

"Wow," she exclaimed as her fingers flew over the keyboard. "Looks like Chris left me three messages." Her face lit up as she bent forward to read them.

Elizabeth felt her heart constrict as she looked at the happy expression on Daphne's face. Was it really possible that less than twenty-four hours ago, she'd had the same look on her own face when she was in Sam's arms? How could things have changed so drastically in such a short time?

Elizabeth shook her head in an effort to clear away the disturbing thoughts that were crowding her brain. She decided to follow Daphne's example and logged on to the computer next to her. *Maybe Nina sent me a message,* she thought as she typed in her password.

Sure enough, there were two messages from Nina. Elizabeth smiled as she scanned the list to see who else had written to her.

Sam.

Elizabeth froze, her heart in her throat. He'd sent it in the middle of the night. Where had he sent it from? she wondered. Did he stop for a cup of coffee at some cybercafé? Had he been at O'Hare? Had he stood at the very same console she was at now?

Her fingers trembled as she clicked on the mouse to read the message. She closed her eyes for a second, trying to gather strength. She knew there was nothing he could say that could make her feel better. Nothing would ever erase the sight of him making out with her sister, his hands all over her. And nothing could make up for his lack of explanation last night. He'd only apologized and then had run off into the night as if he was relieved he'd been caught.

But that he'd made the effort to try to explain, to beg forgiveness, would at least give Elizabeth a small sense of closure.

She slowly opened her eyes and read the message.

Liz,
  Sorry.
     —Sam

Elizabeth blinked in disbelief. She had to be imagining things, but the pathetic message was still there when she opened her eyes. *Sorry.*

What was he thinking? *Sorry* just didn't cut it. If he'd told her that he was joining a monastery or had been banished to a penal colony, she just might consider forgiving him in another fifty years' time. But *sorry?* What planet was he living on? Elizabeth deleted the message and double clicked on the block-sender icon. She never wanted to hear from him again.

She paused for a second, unsure of what she should do next. Her mind was in turmoil. Should she write him a scathing reply? What could she do to let him know how much he'd hurt her?

Nothing. He clearly didn't care about her at all.

"So are you gonna check out the University of London's Web site?" Daphne asked, peeking over at the screen. "I'd love to see what it looks like."

Elizabeth blinked. She had told Daphne about

her acceptance to the school on the ride over to the airport, and Daphne's excitement had helped Elizabeth to forget about her troubles for a while. Now, as thoughts of her new school filled her mind, Sam was once again pushed out. Elizabeth pulled her acceptance letter from her backpack and typed in the Web-site address from the envelope.

When the pictures of the campus appeared, Elizabeth gasped. It was gorgeous! The University of London looked like something out of a fairy tale. The dark gray stone buildings with Gothic towers and mullioned windows were about as far from Sweet Valley's sunny southern California locale as she could imagine. She could almost imagine herself there, walking under the ivy-covered bridges, sitting in classrooms filled with British students, spending afternoons poring over the books in the library—

"Ooh, is that the campus?" Daphne's voice interrupted her thoughts. She leaned over and looked at the screen with a curious expression on her face.

"It's so beautiful," Elizabeth said, touching the screen with a tentative finger. As she did, Daphne stole a glance at her watch.

"Omigod!" Daphne yelped. "My plane is probably boarding!" She jumped up, grabbed her knapsack, and gave Elizabeth a quick kiss on the cheek. "Take care, Elizabeth, and good luck!"

Elizabeth watched her only connection to the

world disappear down the motorized walkway. "You too," she whispered.

She turned back to look at the screen. London was there, waiting for her . . . if only she had the courage to go. Not only the University of London, but the theaters of the West End, the castles and cathedrals, the cozy tea shops and hip pubs, the gardens and literary landmarks . . . the home of her beloved Jane Austen and Emily Brontë and Chaucer and Shakespeare . . . a world she knew only from books and television was just within her reach. . . .

With a burst of energy Elizabeth hoisted her backpack on her shoulder and hurried back toward the British Airways counter. She'd deal with her money situation later. Right now she had a ticket to buy.

"I'd like a one-way ticket to London, please," she said to the ticket agent when she reached the front of the line. She withdrew her credit card from her wallet and placed it and her passport on the counter. "And I'd like to check my duffel."

"The fare is still the same," the ticket agent—the same woman she'd spoken to earlier that morning—informed Elizabeth with a sympathetic expression.

"That's fine," Elizabeth said as confidently as she could. She was surprised that her voice could be heard over the beating of her heart.

Good-bye, America. Hello, London.

Chapter Four

What can I possibly say to them? Jessica wondered as she stared at the phone in the lobby of the motel. *Hey, Mom, hey, Dad, listen, um, Elizabeth caught me making out with her boyfriend, and naturally she wasn't too thrilled about it, so she cut out with the Jeep, and I don't have any bucks. And did I mention I'm somewhere in Illinois? So, uh, feel like bailing me out?*

Yeah, right. Jessica could more than imagine what the reaction on the other end of the phone would be like. After her father finished reviving her mother from a dead faint, Jessica would have some pretty fancy explaining to do.

One thing was for sure—there was no way she could tell them the truth. Not if she wanted them to help her. Well, they'd help her; they were her parents, but not until they'd screamed at her six ways from Sunday first. On the other hand, if she told them a slightly doctored version of the truth, well, then they'd scream at *Elizabeth* six ways from Sunday.

Jessica took a deep breath. Her hand trembled as she picked up the receiver, and she paused to gather her courage before punching in the numbers. If only there were another way out of the situation. But she'd gone over every possible scenario in her mind, and she kept coming up blank.

Jessica leaned back in the booth and stared out the glass doors as she waited to be connected to the operator. She could see that Larry was totally into the blonde. *I wonder if she's trying to flirt her way out of paying* her *bill,* Jessica thought as she watched the way the girl flipped her ponytail. If she was, then she was clearly having more luck than Jessica. Larry was totally into her. He appeared to be oblivious to everything else.

Wait a minute! Jessica slammed down the receiver and sat bolt upright. There *was* another way out of her situation.

She opened the door a crack and peered out. She couldn't hear everything that Larry was saying, but it was clear that he was totally into the conversation and wouldn't be coming up for air anytime soon.

Jessica sat back, her mind working furiously. Would Larry notice if she just snuck out of the lobby? The way he was going, he probably wouldn't miss her until she was across the state line.

Could she do it? Jessica pushed down the twinges of guilt she was feeling about stiffing the motel. Well, what *else* could she do? It wasn't as if she had the money. Besides, if she ran now, she'd be leaving all her clothes behind, and her DKNY mock-croc skirt was worth at least as much as the bill.

Of course I don't know how Larry would look in turquoise. Jessica giggled to herself, feeling like some of her old bravado was returning.

Okay, this was it—now or never. Jessica opened the door as quietly as she could manage and poked her head out. Larry didn't even notice. She stepped out of the booth and began to walk stealthily across the lobby.

Okay, keep it going; everything's cool; the door's only about two yards away—

"Hey! Where're you sneaking off to?" Larry's voice cut through the air like a buzz saw.

Cold sweat broke out on Jessica's forehead as she started to run toward the door. She shoved past an elderly couple and jumped down the steps, miserably aware that Larry was gaining on her.

"Hey, you're not leaving here without paying!" Larry yelled as he ran after her.

"That's what you think," Jessica whispered as she ran. She was almost off the property now, and if she could just make it to the highway, she could hitch a ride and be home free.

She raced across the lawn like an Olympic hurdler, jumping over the flower beds and skirting past the deck chairs.

Almost there, Jessica thought, panting as she ran. She could see the cars on the highway and imagined how good she'd feel once she was on her way and she could begin putting the whole nightmare behind her.

"Just a few more—ahhh!" Jessica yelled in pain as she tripped over a coiled-up garden hose and collapsed on the hard asphalt that bordered the lawn. "Ow!"

She grabbed her ankle as she crumpled up in a little ball. She'd never been in so much pain in her life. Her ankle was definitely sprained, perhaps even broken. *Just a few feet away from freedom and I crash,* she thought mournfully.

"Not so fast," Larry said as he came puffing up behind her. He laid a heavy hand on her arm as if he was afraid she'd try to bolt again. "You're not going anywhere until you've paid your bill."

"This has to be, like, the oldest trick in the book," Larry grumbled to Jessica as he pulled his beat-up Honda outside the door to the emergency room at the local hospital. "I mean, a broken ankle?" He sneered. "Why didn't you try for something really dramatic, like a coma or something?"

"It's not an act," Jessica said, gritting her teeth. She wasn't sure which was bothering her more: the shooting pains in her ankle or Larry's snide remarks.

The past twenty minutes in the car with him had been about the most unpleasant that she could remember. He'd spent the entire time complaining about having to get Joe, the night manager, to cover for him at the motel. "Now I owe him a favor, and that's exactly what I don't need," he kept muttering, along with ragging on her about the bill and stopping only to tease her mercilessly about her accident, which he was sure she'd faked. She couldn't believe that she'd ever even *tried* to flirt with him. Eww!

I must be having a nightmare, Jessica thought as she looked out at the hospital's grim industrial exterior. That must be the explanation for her current predicament. She refused to believe that her life could have taken such a turn for the worse in less than twenty-four hours. But then again, would her ankle hurt so much if she were asleep?

No, she was definitely awake; the problem was

that she'd clearly stepped on the express elevator to hell.

"No one said that you had to drive me to the hospital," Jessica muttered under her breath. She struggled to open the door handle, but it was stuck, and she leaned back in the seat, exhausted. She didn't have the energy to get out of the car.

"Are you kidding?" Larry said, laughing as he stepped nimbly out of the car and walked around to the passenger's side. "I want to see for myself just how bad this 'broken ankle' really is. Besides, there's no way I'm letting you out of my sight. You're not stiffing the motel during my shift, lady." He opened the passenger door, and Jessica tumbled out.

"Ow!" Jessica nearly doubled over in agony as her foot touched the pavement; a shaft of pain burned through her leg. "You'd better get me a wheelchair," she whispered, grimacing with each red-hot pinprick.

Larry rolled his eyes and retrieved a wheelchair from just inside the lobby, his eyes, as promised, never leaving Jessica. "I'll say this much," he commented as he helped Jessica into the chair. "You sure are a good actress. You looked like you were going to keel over for a second there."

"That's because I *was* about to keel over," Jessica hissed as he wheeled her into the emergency room. Thankfully there were only two other people waiting, neither of them looking as dire as she was sure she did.

The nurse behind the admitting desk barely glanced up as they approached. She had curly blond hair and a large chest, something that Jessica saw Larry take an immediate note of. Ugh.

"It's my ankle," Jessica began softly, hoping that no one would think that she and Larry were, well, *together*.

The nurse frowned and leaned over the desk. "You'll have to speak up, miss. Whispering will get you nowhere."

Gee, I wonder if she's always this friendly, Jessica thought. Weren't nurses supposed to be kind and sympathetic?

"I think I broke my ankle," Jessica bit out as a searing pain shot up her leg.

"Well, in that case you'll need to have an x ray taken," the nurse said briskly, tucking a stray curl behind her ear. "I'll need your insurance card, please." She extended her hand.

"Insurance card?" Jessica repeated. She'd forgotten that things like x rays and medical care cost money—probably even more than motel bills.

"If you don't have one, you'll have to pay for your treatment by cash or credit card," the nurse said, eyeing her.

51

"Of course I have an insurance card!" Jessica said hotly.

"Ha!" Larry snickered. He leaned forward and spoke to the nurse confidentially. "Take it from me—you better make sure that she pays up front."

"Thank you for your concern, sir." The nurse turned to Jessica. "If you'll give me your card, we can begin filling out the necessary paperwork."

"Well, I—," Jessica began.

"What do you bet she claims she lost it?" Larry interrupted, sidling away from the wheelchair and inching toward the nurse. "Go on," Larry urged. "I can't wait to hear this. I could use a good laugh."

Jessica stared helplessly back and forth between the two of them.

"Miss, I don't have all day," the nurse said, her civil tone souring.

"Well?" Larry prodded. "Did you lose it?"

"I didn't lose my card!" Jessica exclaimed.

And that was true. She knew exactly where it was: safe inside Elizabeth's wallet. "It's just not here right now," she said quietly. "And—and I don't have any cash on me."

"Then I'm sorry, but the official policy of the hospital is no medical treatment without a valid insurance card or cash payment up front." The nurse gave a brief, sympathetic smile, then went back to her paperwork.

"But—But you can't just deny someone in pain treatment, can you?" Jessica asked fearfully. "That's—That's inhumane!"

"Look, miss, I'm sorry, but I'm just the messenger," the nurse said in an even tone, as if she'd given this speech before. "Now, you'd best be on your way, or I'll have to call security, which I would just hate to do." She looked past Jessica and motioned with her hand. "Sir? Can I help you?" A twenty-something man with a bloody gash in his arm moved to the desk.

Okay, now I know I'm having a nightmare. Jessica groaned to herself, burying her head in her hands. She licked her lips, trying to ignore the pain—and Larry's evil eye. What could she do?

She *couldn't* call her parents. She'd already considered that scenario back at the motel. Besides, they were in Sweet Valley, California, halfway across the country. What could *they* do?

There was one other person she could call.

Elizabeth. But Jessica doubted there would be anything but ice in her sister's voice. *If* Elizabeth would even speak to her.

Was it awful to call Elizabeth to ask for her insurance-card number? Maybe Elizabeth would feel so bad for her that she'd come back. Jessica sincerely doubted that, but it was the only chance she had.

"I need to make a phone call," she said wearily.

"See," Larry told the nurse. "This is how she operates. She'll try and make a break for it."

"I don't think she'll get very far in the shape she's in," the nurse replied. "The phones are over there." She pointed toward the corner.

"Thank you," Jessica said as she dropped down into the wheelchair and wheeled herself toward the nearest phone. Her hands were shaking so badly that she couldn't get a hold on the receiver. She wiped her hands on her pants.

Get a grip, she told herself. She tried to take several calming deep breaths, but she was having a hard time controlling her rising panic. However much she wanted to believe that Elizabeth was going to come and save her, she had an uncomfortable feeling that things were about to get even nastier.

In fact, the more she thought about it, the more it seemed like Larry and the nurse were just the opening act for what promised to be a truly unpleasant showdown with her sister.

Chapter Five

Elizabeth popped a french fry into her mouth as she leaned back against the red leather booth. She'd dialed home four times, but the line was busy. Her dad probably had one of his clients on the phone, which meant she could have a very long wait ahead of her. So, she'd found a table at one of the cheaper airport restaurants and ordered a side of fries and a vanilla milk shake. "This might be the last milk shake I have for a long time," she said to herself as she tore the wrapper off her straw. Did they have milk shakes in England? Or did everyone just drink tea? "Maybe I should get a Coke and a burger too," she added jokingly under her breath. Fish-and-chips shops were probably more plentiful than burger joints. And didn't they use vinegar instead of ketchup?

She laughed for what seemed like the first time

in days. Here she was, about to leave her country, her home, and everything that was familiar to her, and she was stressing about whether or not her new life would have ketchup in it.

Just then a familiar buzzing interrupted her thoughts. She reached into her backpack for her cell phone and stared at the telephone number on the display. She didn't recognize it, and she paused before flipping open the phone. What if it was Sam? Her stomach clenched at the thought. What would she do? No doubt she'd start crying all over again, but what about after that? Should she hang up on him, or should she yell at him first? Elizabeth didn't think that she could possibly begin to tell him how much he'd hurt her . . . and she didn't really feel like exposing herself that deeply to someone who so obviously cared so little. No, if it was Sam, she'd just hang up.

On the other hand, maybe it would be Nina. Elizabeth longed to hear a sympathetic voice, and there was a good chance that Nina would call her from work and Elizabeth wouldn't recognize that number. Hoping it was her friend, she flipped open the phone.

"Hello?" Elizabeth asked as she swallowed some milk shake. She frowned at the staticky silence on the other end. "Hello?" she repeated tentatively.

A computer-operated voice came on the line. "You have a collect call from Jessica Wakefield. Will you accept the charges?"

Elizabeth stared at the phone. Was it some kind of joke?

Jessica was calling to apologize, of course. She'd try to get back into Elizabeth's good graces. Tell her that Sam was a no-good cheat, just like she'd been telling Elizabeth during the entire trip. That she was so sorry for going after him, but she couldn't help developing feelings for Sam, and she suddenly realized her sister was more important than some guy.

"Sorry, Jess," Elizabeth half whispered. "I'm through giving you second chances."

The computer-operated voice repeated its message. "You have a collect call from Jessica Wakefield. Will you accept the charges?"

"I'm sorry," Elizabeth managed to croak. "But you must have the wrong number. I don't know any Jessica Wakefield."

Her hands were shaking uncontrollably as she snapped the phone shut. *What was Jessica going to say to me?* Elizabeth wondered. She felt sick all over again. She pushed away her plate, her appetite suddenly gone. Elizabeth almost felt a twinge of regret. Maybe she should have accepted the call.

No. Elizabeth had done the right thing. Even if Jessica apologized into the next millennium,

Elizabeth would never be able to forgive her. Still, it would be nice to know that she was at least feeling a little remorseful.

Elizabeth sighed. Who was she kidding? Knowing that Jessica was sorry for what she'd done wouldn't make her feel any better. Maybe if she knew that the rest of Jessica's life was ruined, or at least the next five years, now *that* might do it.

As Elizabeth turned off the phone's ringer and tucked it away into the zippered pocket of her backpack, her hand closed around the hard edge of a book. What was it? Elizabeth didn't remember packing any hardcovers. She pulled out the book and stared at the blue leather cover.

"My journal," Elizabeth murmured. She must be even further gone than she thought to have forgotten about her journal. Elizabeth was amazed that she hadn't thought of it before. She opened it up on the table and reached into her backpack for a pen. No matter what, she'd always have her journal.

The words flowed fast and furious as she started to write. She poured out her heart onto the crisp white pages. Some of the pain seemed to seep out of her bones, and she relaxed for the first time in hours as she tried to make sense of what had happened to her.

"Mind if I sit here?"

Elizabeth looked up, startled. *What is it with this city? Can't a girl just sit by herself? And just when I was getting into it too,* she thought, irritated at the interruption.

A tall, good-looking guy was staring at her as if she was the best thing that he'd seen in days. He was wearing a cowboy hat and a cocky grin. Even if Elizabeth hadn't sworn off men for the rest of the century, she wouldn't have been into him. He looked like the kind of guy who thought that women existed only to serve him, and Elizabeth didn't feel like raising his feminist consciousness.

She looked around and was relieved to see that there were plenty of empty tables—that way she wouldn't feel bad telling him to park his spurs somewhere else.

"Uh, sorry." Elizabeth closed her journal so he couldn't see what she was writing. "But there are lots of free tables here, and I'm really trying to concentrate."

"It's true that there are a lot of other tables," he drawled. "But this is the only one with a bodacious blonde."

Oh, brother. Elizabeth rolled her eyes. Where'd he dig that one up? Some guide to dating written by a computer nerd back in the eighties?

"So, blondie," the cowboy continued. "What do you say you and me get to know each other a little better?" He started to sit down.

What's wrong with this lug? Elizabeth thought, grimacing. *Any fool could pick up on my coldness. I'm so not into this right now!* Even if she hadn't just lost her boyfriend, she wouldn't give this guy the time of day.

"Sorry, guy, but she's with me," said a cultured, British-accented voice.

Elizabeth turned around to see a guy her age standing next to the table. He looked like a young Ralph Fiennes, and he was holding two cups of coffee and a plate of English muffins. He smiled at her, and Elizabeth wasn't sure, but she thought she saw a sly wink.

The cowboy sized up Ralph, gave him a dirty look, then thankfully sauntered away.

"Thanks," Elizabeth said to the Ralph lookalike. She offered him a smile, which seemed to give him the encouragement to sit down opposite her. He slid one of his coffees her way.

Yes, he was cute. Very cute. And he'd done her a huge favor. But she wanted him to beat it too. All she wanted to do was write in her journal and see if she could make some sense out of the dramatic turn her life had taken. Was there a polite way to ask him to leave also? She didn't think so. And besides, he *had* helped her out with the cowboy.

"No problem," he said. "I saw him bothering you, and I figured that I could offer my services. He didn't look like the kind of bloke you wanted to be messing about with." He flashed her a grin. "But you have no idea how effective an English accent can be. People tend to imagine that you're fearfully upper crust and get intimidated intellectually."

Elizabeth smiled, then couldn't help herself. She laughed. In spite of herself she was almost interested. Was it fate that this guy was British? Was it an omen that an Englishman had rescued her? Whatever, she was fascinated by the way he spoke. And what did *bloke* mean anyway?

"My name's Nigel," he said. "And you are . . . ?"

"Elizabeth."

She felt slightly overwhelmed by his very correct British manner. She couldn't imagine Sam Burgess ever overwhelming anyone with his manner, which had been pure rude. Of course Nigel was helped by the fact that he was wearing a very correct blazer with what she guessed was a school insignia embroidered on the pocket—Sam usually had a baseball cap on backward and a Road Runner T-shirt stained with the last few meals he'd eaten.

What did I see in Sam anyway? Elizabeth wondered. She sighed deeply. In spite of the fact that he'd been rude and sloppy, he was one of the most brilliant guys she'd ever been with. Would she ever meet anyone else that she enjoyed talking to as much? Would she ever meet anyone else that she enjoyed kissing as much? Somehow Elizabeth had a feeling that it didn't really matter because she couldn't imagine ever being that close to anyone again.

"I bought two cups of coffee since one cup's never enough," Nigel said, flashing a dimple. "Being a Brit, I'm a tea drinker, of course, but a semester abroad in America, and I'm addicted to Starbucks."

Elizabeth laughed. How good it felt!

"The crumpets aren't the same, though," Nigel lamented.

Crumpets? Elizabeth shook her head in amusement as she tried to decipher Nigel's words. Since he had an English muffin in front of him, she had to assume that English muffins were called crumpets in England.

Suddenly Elizabeth felt a little nervous. It had never occurred to her that English people spoke differently than she did. After all, they both spoke, well, *English.* But after just a few seconds of talking to Nigel she realized that while the English spoken by the *English* wasn't Swahili, it wasn't exactly the same as what she was used to hearing back in southern California. Elizabeth accepted one of the English muffins that Nigel offered her and put away her journal. She still wished that she could just sit by herself and write, but she had more important things to do now.

After all, if I'm going to feel at home with the natives, I better learn the language, Elizabeth thought, grinning at her new friend.

Chapter
Six

_____

Jessica stared at the phone as if it had bitten her. She couldn't believe what had just happened. Yeah, she'd figured it wouldn't be a bed of roses. She'd braced herself to hear Elizabeth shriek at her, she'd been ready to have insults hurled her way, she'd expected pain and sadness in her sister's voice, but she never, never thought that Elizabeth would make good on her threat.

You're not my sister anymore. . . .

Jessica replaced the receiver and buried her face in her hands. She couldn't stop replaying Elizabeth's curt response over and over again in her mind. *I don't know any Jessica Wakefield.* Every time she repeated the words, she flinched as if she'd been slapped. She'd thought that after what she'd been through in the past twenty-four hours, nothing could ever hurt her again. Well, she was wrong.

Elizabeth's words had sliced through her like a knife, shredding what was left of her heart. In spite of everything that had happened, Jessica had held on to the belief that at some point she and Elizabeth would be able to work things out. But now she wondered whether that could really happen. It seemed that as far as Elizabeth was concerned, Jessica didn't even exist.

Don't be such an idiot, Jessica told herself. *It was only last night that it happened. Only last night that Elizabeth saw you in the arms of her boyfriend. You can't expect her to forgive you overnight.*

Still, Jessica couldn't stop wondering, believing, even, that Elizabeth would forgive her if she knew what kind of situation she was in now.

Jessica looked back toward the nurses' station. Larry and the nurse seemed extra cozy together now. The nurse was still busy with her paperwork, but she was laughing at something Larry had said. There was no way that Jessica could bring herself to go back there and tell them that she didn't have her insurance card and that she had no way of paying for the treatment she so desperately needed.

Larry watched with narrowed eyes as Jessica picked up the phone once again. She was a master at getting herself out of sticky situations, but this time her imagination failed her. She ran over a variety of possible scenarios in her head as she dialed the operator.

I guess I'll just leave out the juicy parts, she thought, biting her cuticles. As the collect call was put through, Jessica started chewing like crazy.

"Hello?"

Jessica almost sobbed in relief as her mother's soft voice floated across the phone lines.

"Mom?" she wailed. She knew she sounded like a little girl again, but she didn't care.

"Jessica?" Her mother was instantly alert. "Is something wrong?"

Try everything. Jessica didn't know where to begin. "I . . . I broke my ankle," she blurted out.

"How? Where are you, honey?" Alice Wakefield's tone was full of compassion.

Jessica closed her eyes. Just the sound of her voice was reassuring. She was the first person who hadn't yelled at Jessica in hours.

"What happened, sweetie?" Mrs. Wakefield asked. "Are you in a hospital? Are you sure it's broken?"

"Yes, I'm in the hospital, but I, uh . . . well, it's kind of complicated. . . ." Jessica's voice trailed away. The initial pleasure of talking to her mother was wearing off, and she was left with the fact that she had some pretty fancy explaining to do.

"Do you need to rest? Are you in too much

pain to talk?" her mom asked. "Put Elizabeth on the phone. Let me talk to her."

Jessica squirmed in her wheelchair. "Um, I can't really do that, Mom."

"Why not? Where is she?" Her mom sounded confused. "Is she getting you something to eat?"

"Uh, n-not exactly," Jessica stammered. *Here goes,* she thought, taking a deep breath. "We kind of had a fight. I guess we shouldn't have driven cross-country together." Jessica's voice grew more confident as the words tumbled out. "We were at each other's throats the whole time." That wasn't true, but Jessica had to say something. "Things got sort of out of hand. . . ."

"I don't understand," her mom said. "Didn't Elizabeth come with you to the hospital?"

Yes, Mom, that's exactly what I'm saying, Jessica answered mentally, tears stinging the backs of her eyes. *And, um, if I told you why, you'd hate my guts, just like Elizabeth does.*

You're not my daughter anymore. . . .

Sorry, Operator, but I can't accept the charges. I don't have a daughter named Jessica. . . .

Jessica squeezed her eyes shut and felt a sob rise in her throat. "No, Mom, Elizabeth didn't come with me," she whispered. "I don't know where she is."

Suddenly it was all too much. Overwhelmed by everything, by what had happened last night, what

66

had happened this morning, Larry staring at her with his evil eye, and her mother asking questions that Jessica couldn't bear to answer, the tears came. Sobs racked Jessica's body in the wheelchair.

"What?" her mom asked. "What do you mean?"

Well, you see, Mom, she was about to have sex with this total jerk loser, and I just couldn't bear for Elizabeth to give up her virginity to some cheating liar, so I had to stop her. And I did. You'd have been really proud of me. I saved her from making the biggest mistake of her life. How? Oh, uh, well, I pretended to be her and started making out with Sam, and I arranged it so she'd see us, and she flipped, like I expected.

But she took off, like I didn't expect.

I'm not sure what I expected, actually.

Jessica doubled over in tears, clutching the phone to her ear as if it were a lifeline.

"Jessica, I want you to calm down and tell me where Elizabeth is," her mom said, her tone changing from calm to upset.

"She left," Jessica whispered, wiping the tears from under her eyes. She sniffled. "She's gone. She drove away in the Jeep, and I haven't seen her since last night."

"Jessica?" Her father's voice came on the line. Jessica could just picture him picking up the phone in his study and listening in, a worried frown distorting his handsome face. Relief poured through her. Even though she was completely torn up over what had happened with Elizabeth, now that her parents were in the picture, she felt like the nightmare was coming to an end. At least she wouldn't be alone and penniless anymore. At least her parents would take care of her. "Jessica, where are you?" her dad asked.

Jessica sniffled. "Um, I don't know. Somewhere in Illinois."

"Honey, ask the nurse or doctor what town," her mom said.

Jessica glanced up. A young girl and her mother were sitting near the phone.

"Um, excuse me?" she whispered loudly. "Could you tell me what town we're in?"

The girl giggled as her mom said, "Springfield."

"I'm in Springfield," Jessica managed to croak into the phone.

"We heard," Mr. Wakefield said, his voice gruff. "The minute the doctor is finished bandaging you up, I want you to take a cab to the airport and get on a plane home. We'll pick you up at the airport, and—"

"Um, Dad," Jessica began, closing her eyes and gearing up for what she had to say, "I, um, uh, I don't have my insurance card, and I only have a few bucks on me, and, um, I exceeded the credit limit on my Visa, and so the hospital hasn't taken any x rays or anything yet—"

"What?" Mrs. Wakefield said. "Jessica, where is your insurance card?"

"Um, Elizabeth has it?" Jessica asked more than said.

"I'm confused," her father cut in. "*Where* did you say Elizabeth was, exactly?"

Jessica sighed. "We got into a fight, and she took off in the Jeep, and I haven't seen her since last night, and, um, I sort of owe a lot of money at the motel too, and—"

"That doesn't sound like Elizabeth," Mrs. Wakefield said.

"No, it doesn't," Mr. Wakefield echoed.

"Are you saying that Elizabeth stranded you in the middle of Illinois with no car, no money, no insurance card, and a hotel bill?" her mother asked.

"Um, yes," Jessica whispered. *Just bail me out,* she prayed silently. *Stop asking questions and please bail me out.*

"Well, I don't understand any of this," her dad said. Jessica could tell her father had put his hand over the receiver so that she couldn't hear what he was saying to her mother. She heard some garbled voices. "Jessica, listen to me," her dad said. "Your mom and I are going to fly out to Springfield. Hang tight, and we should be there in a couple of hours, okay?"

"Okay." Jessica sniffed. She knew a last-minute flight was going to cost her parents a fortune, but right now, she didn't care. She needed them.

"Now, put the admitting nurse on the phone, and we'll take care of the insurance information so you can be treated."

Jessica couldn't speak. She could only nod.

Everything's going to be okay, Jessica told herself. She told her parents to hold the line, then let the receiver drop and dangle as she wheeled herself over to the admittance desk.

"My parents would like to talk to you, Nurse," Jessica said. "They have my insurance-card number."

"All right, then," the woman said curtly, heading toward the pay phone with her clipboard.

"They'd better have a credit-card number too," Larry added, tapping his pudgy fingers on the counter. "Or else I'm calling the police."

Ignoring him, Jessica wheeled herself over to the waiting area. *Things are going to work out just fine,* Jessica reassured herself, but somehow even the thought of her parents taking charge failed to comfort her. Because deep inside, Jessica knew that something had changed forever. Maybe they could deal with her motel bill and get her ankle patched up. But who would patch her up inside? Who would make things better between her and Elizabeth?

It's going to take a long, long time to fix things up with Elizabeth, she thought, wiping the tears from her face with the back of her hand. *That's if they ever get fixed at all.*

Chapter
Seven

Nigel was flirting with Elizabeth. Big-time flirting. And she was big-time *not* interested. She wondered if she'd ever be interested in having a relationship with anyone ever again.

"I'm sorry, I didn't hear what you were saying," Elizabeth said, putting down her cell phone. "It's just that I need to reach my parents, and my dad's cell is busy." When she had pulled her cell phone out of her backpack to call her house again, there were no messages from Jessica—but there were *three* from her parents. That could mean only one thing. Jessica had called them. Elizabeth had listened to the messages, both delivered in the same anxious tone. *Elizabeth, this is your mother. Call us immediately on your father's cell.*

Elizabeth took a deep breath. What had Jessica told them? And why had she bothered them anyway?

Granted, Elizabeth had stranded her in the motel, but Jessica had credit cards and some cash. It wasn't like she was completely helpless. Then Elizabeth had a sudden, uneasy thought. Could Jessica be in O'Hare as well, waiting for a plane back to Sweet Valley? Was her twin here too?

She gave Nigel a small smile as she finished the last of her English muffin. Although at first she'd been happy that Nigel had chased the cowboy away, the charm of having to make polite conversation when she was feeling so overwrought was starting to wear thin.

Nigel was nice, but he just didn't seem to take the hint. He kept asking her questions and talking about himself. Ordinarily Elizabeth would have welcomed the opportunity to talk to a British guy her own age; after all, she had loads of her own questions about the country she'd be living in for a semester. Plus she and Nigel did have a lot in common. He'd mentioned that he planned to be a writer and was involved in an English-literature program at Cambridge. Elizabeth was sure they had plenty to talk about, but right now she had too much on her mind.

Without exactly knowing why, Elizabeth picked up her cell to try again, then slowly put it down. She knew she should keep trying to reach them— her mom had sounded so urgent. But it was one thing to call and tell them she was going to go to the University of London on a full scholarship. It was another thing to call and tell them what had gone down between her and Jessica. She wasn't looking forward to that at all.

"I was telling you about the reading room at the British Library," Nigel said, running a hand through his thick, brown hair. "Although you'll probably want to see the major attractions first. The Tower of London, Big Ben, Westminster Abbey . . ." He went on, naming all the London landmarks Elizabeth had dreamed her whole life about seeing.

"Right," Elizabeth murmured absentmindedly. A young woman who reminded her so much of Jessica that it made her throat ache caught her eye. She had the same long, blond hair and carefree style that Jessica had. Even her clothing sense was the same— the sleeveless hot pink shirt, white shorts, and matching sandals she wore were right up Jessica's sexy alley.

"Have you ever tried it?" Nigel asked.

Elizabeth blinked and glanced at Nigel. "Um, I'm sorry, tried what?"

"Cucumber sandwiches," Nigel said, a bit impatiently. "I've been talking about them for the last five minutes. Well, not that cucumber sandwiches are that interesting," he added, that perfect dimple reappearing in his cheek.

"Oh, right," Elizabeth said. "Cucumber sand-wiches." She nodded as if she understood what he was talking about, trying to look like she was pay-ing attention. Then she glanced at the large clock overhead. If she was going to go to London today, time to reach her parents was running out. What if she didn't reach them before she left and ended up on a jet bound for England without them even knowing it? Or what if she did reach them but got stuck explaining everything to them on the phone and missed her flight? Then what would she do? Panic began settling into Elizabeth's stomach.

"Well, after you try a cucumber sandwich at a tea, you should pop over to Madame Tussaud's," Nigel said with a smile. "It's a wax museum. They have wax figures of everyone—Madonna, Elvis Presley, Prince William too, I think."

"Wow. That sounds . . . um, fun." Elizabeth knew that she was being rude, and it was clear from the look on Nigel's face that he thought so too. He looked slightly put out, and Elizabeth felt a flash of guilt. He'd only tried to be nice to her, and here she was, hurting his feelings. But what could she do? She had a lot more important things on her mind than some jewels and a bunch of wax dummies.

Wait a minute, Elizabeth thought, sitting up sharply. What was she doing, worrying about some stranger's feelings? Weren't her *own* more important? Maybe the old Elizabeth would sit and listen to some guy ramble on, cute or not, but the new Elizabeth wasn't going to be anybody's doormat. She had her *own* feelings to worry about. She didn't need to stress on Nigel's.

Would the kind of girl who traveled halfway around the world at a moment's notice sit and listen to someone when she had other things to do? Would the kind of girl who had the courage to fly off to London with barely any cash and not much more than that in the way of luggage put a stranger's needs before her own? Elizabeth didn't think so for a second, and she was bound and determined to be that other type of girl.

"It's been really nice talking to you, Nigel," Elizabeth said, bolting up and reaching for her backpack. "But I'd better get going. I have some stuff to do before my plane leaves." *Like returning my parents' call and telling them I'm leaving for London tonight*.

Once she was safely out of Nigel's view, Elizabeth found an empty seat in the British Airways departure area. She smoothed some of the wrinkles out of her jeans as she perched on her chair and punched in the number again. This time there was no busy signal.

As she waited anxiously for her dad to answer,

Elizabeth tucked a limp lock of hair behind her ear. What she wouldn't give for a hot shower! She supposed that would have to wait until she was settled in her dorm room in England. Elizabeth smiled at the thought. She was going to study abroad—in London! In spite of all the heartache she'd experienced in the last twenty-four hours, it was hard not to feel just a tiny bit excited.

"Hello?" Alice Wakefield's voice floated across the phone lines, jarring Elizabeth back to the present.

"Hi, Mom," Elizabeth said, feeling an unexpected pang of sadness, knowing that she wouldn't be seeing her for months. Before she could say another word, her dad came on the line.

"Elizabeth, is that you?"

"Yes, Daddy, it's me."

"Where are you?"

"At O'Hare," Elizabeth said, just as a British Airways flight to Heathrow Airport was called over the loudspeaker. "It's kind of a long story—"

"O'Hare?" her dad repeated. "What in heaven's name are you doing at the airport? *You* have the Jeep."

Elizabeth frowned. Why did her dad sound so angry? *It must just be my imagination*, Elizabeth reassured herself. She was so tired and worn out that she was starting to get paranoid. Unless Jessica had twisted everything when she called them. If she'd called them, that was.

"Elizabeth?" her dad barked. "Answer me, please."

Elizabeth blinked in surprise. She wasn't paranoid. Her parents were angry—unmistakably angry. What was going on? "Did you guys speak to Jessica? Because if you did, I'm sure she—"

"Yes, we just got off the phone with your sister. She's hurt and confused, and frankly, so are we," her dad said. "Your mother and I would like to know what possessed you to strand your sister with a broken ankle, no money, and no insurance card in the middle of nowhere?"

Elizabeth heard the muffled tones of her mother asking for the phone. "Elizabeth," her mom began, sounding on the verge of tears, "I don't understand. How could you have done that to Jessica? How could you be so indifferent and so cruel?"

Whaaa? Elizabeth was shocked. How could she have done *what* to Jessica? And what broken ankle? What kind of nonsense had Jessica been spinning? And why had her parents so clearly bought it? Major, *major* damage control was in order.

"Against our better judgment, we trusted you girls not only with the Jeep, but to drive cross-country," her mom went on, almost more to herself than to Elizabeth. "I don't know what caused your argument, but certainly nothing is worth abandoning each other in a strange place, especially when Jessica needed medical care."

"Mom, wait a minute—"

"Your mother is too upset to talk," her dad said as he got back on the phone.

"I didn't leave Jessica with a broken ankle," Elizabeth replied lamely. She couldn't believe that her parents would think she'd do such a thing. And who cared about a stupid ankle? A busted ankle would heal. But what Jessica had done to her would never, ever heal.

Just when Elizabeth had found something special with Sam, Jessica had to ruin everything. Sure, Sam was obviously no prize, but did her own twin have to be the one to show her that? Because of Jessica, Elizabeth's life would never be the same. Clearly her sister hadn't breathed a word of what had happened. Elizabeth started to burn as she thought of the injustice.

And Mom and Dad are mad at me? Elizabeth clenched the phone so tightly that her knuckles turned white. "I don't think you have the whole story," she said thickly, trying to ignore the rowdy group of men sitting across from her. "I don't know what Jessica told you, but—" Elizabeth couldn't stop herself from wailing. "You *have* to believe me. What happened back in Springfield was Jessica's fault."

"I'm not interested in placing blame right now," her father said, his voice angry. "What I am interested in is getting you and your sister home, safe and sound and where you both belong."

But did she? Did she, Elizabeth Wakefield, really belong in Sweet Valley? All of a sudden something snapped inside her. Elizabeth had always been expected to be the good, responsible, mature twin, and she'd done no less. Jessica had always been the flighty and irresponsible one, smiling and conniving her way out of everything. Well, Elizabeth had had it.

Jessica had gone too far this time.

"Dad, I don't belong at home," Elizabeth began slowly. "At least right now. Too much has happened—"

"You can stop with the theatrics," her father snapped into the phone. "I'm not interested in what you think you can or cannot deal with. Frankly, I'm appalled—"

"Stop blaming me!" Elizabeth protested, raising her voice. "I'm not the bad guy here! Stop thinking about Jessica and think about *me* for a change! Think about why I might have left Jessica in that motel! Think about what she must have done!"

"You're acting like a child, Elizabeth," her dad said. "Like a five-year-old instead of a young woman who's about to turn twenty. Do you hear yourself? You've always taken yourself a little too seriously, and it's clear from this situation that—"

And it's clear from this situation that you have no idea who I am, Elizabeth thought. She'd always believed her parents respected her, but it was clear they didn't . . . that when it came down to it, they didn't trust her judgment or her ethics.

They didn't believe in her.

A pain worse than anything she'd ever known sliced through her heart. She'd thought that she'd known heartbreak when she'd seen Sam and Jessica groping each other in the motel. She'd thought that she'd known what it was to be lonely as she wandered around the huge international airport, all alone. Well, she'd been wrong. Having her parents turn on her, doubt her, and stick up for Jessica was the worst pain she'd known yet.

She *was* on her own. She took out the ticket sheaf and pulled out the ticket. She'd tried to do the right thing, tried to share with them the exciting news that she'd be going to London, but if they weren't going to listen . . . if they weren't going to believe in her, well, then . . .

"Now, this is what you're going to do," her father instructed, as if she were one of his office paralegals and not his own flesh and blood. "Get out a pen and some paper because I'm going to give you the address of the Springfield hospital. Leave the Jeep wherever you've parked it, go to the taxi stand, and take a cab directly there," her father told her. "Jessica will probably still be in the ER. On the way there, you can start thinking about the apology you're going to give to her. Your mother and I are going to—" He droned on, but Elizabeth wasn't listening.

An apology? That was the last straw.

Elizabeth stared at her cell phone. Slowly, very slowly, she moved her index finger to the off button. Her finger hovered over it.

"Elizabeth?" she heard her father say. "Did you get all of that?"

She had. She pressed the button.

And for the first time in her entire life, responsible, dependable, good Elizabeth Wakefield hung up on her parents.

Chapter Eight

Elizabeth stared at herself underneath the harsh fluorescent lights of the airport ladies' room. Her eyes were so puffy that they were practically swollen shut, her face was tearstained and blotchy, and her hair looked like straw.

Well, what do I expect? Elizabeth asked herself. *That's what happens when you stay up half the night and cry half the day.*

Elizabeth hadn't stopped crying since she'd hung up on her parents over an hour ago. She hurt much too badly to stop. Of course, it didn't help that people were staring at her as if she were from another planet. Finally she had escaped to the relative privacy of the ladies' room. She'd gotten tired of well-meaning strangers coming up and asking if something was wrong.

Well, guess what, folks, there is something wrong

with me! How would you guys feel if you'd lost your boyfriend, your sister, and your family all at once? She reached into her backpack and took out her comb. She winced as she attempted to drag it through the tangles, then gave up and threw it back inside her pack. Her hair was hopeless. *Everything's hopeless.* Elizabeth teared up again. *My life is hopeless.*

She turned on both taps and ran the water until it was practically freezing, then cupped both her hands and splashed her face half a dozen times. She straightened and looked back in the mirror. The water hadn't helped.

She jumped as the door opened with a bang and a brassy blonde came in. Elizabeth took one look at her and then hid her face as best as she could and busied herself with her backpack.

The blonde looked at her curiously as she whipped out a lipstick. "Take it from me, honey," she said as she pulled off the cap. "He's not worth it." Her voice was surprisingly soft, and she gave Elizabeth a small smile before pursing her lips into an exaggerated pout and applying a rich crimson color.

Elizabeth blinked in surprise. She'd expected the blonde to look at her and hand her a tissue, not offer advice.

"Remember, sweetie," the woman continued,

"whether you're coming or going, you're headed *somewhere,* or you wouldn't be in an airport. Don't let anyone drag you down. Move on, girl!"

Elizabeth gnawed her lower lip and stared at herself in the mirror. She was headed somewhere. She did have the means to get there. Not many means, but enough.

"I don't know if I can," Elizabeth blurted out. How could she move on when she barely had two cents to rub together and no one to turn to?

The blonde turned to face Elizabeth, pointing at her with her tube of lipstick. "Of course you can. Because no matter what, you'll always have yourself. That's what I've learned in my long and interesting life." The blonde chuckled and applied another coat of lipstick.

You always have yourself, Elizabeth repeated to herself, eyeing her reflection. *And no matter what my parents think, I know I can trust myself.*

She gave the blonde a weak smile and reached into her backpack for the acceptance letter to the University of London. She would be okay. She had herself and the scholarship. Once she got to the school, she'd be given a room and placed on the meal plan.

"That a love letter?" The blonde quirked an eyebrow.

"In a way," Elizabeth said, reading over the

details of her scholarship. There it was in black and white. A meal plan, a single room, and a small stipend. Elizabeth smiled at the woman. "Thank you. Thank you for the pep talk. You have no idea how much it helped."

The blonde smiled back.

I'm going to do this! Elizabeth thought. *I'm going to go get on that plane and live in London for an entire semester!*

She practically ran out of the bathroom and down the long corridor to the British Airways waiting area. For five hours Elizabeth had been wandering up and down the walkways, sitting in cheap restaurants and waiting areas, worrying. Worrying for nothing. She had herself. She always had, and she'd never let herself down.

Settled on a stiff fake leather chair in the waiting area, Elizabeth reexamined her ticket, running her hand over the blue-and-red folder as if it possessed magical powers. She still couldn't believe that she'd actually done it. There was no going back now. It was amazing to think that just a few pieces of paper stapled together could have the power to change her life so dramatically.

I just wish I was there already, Elizabeth thought as she ran her fingers distractedly through her hair. Now that she'd finally bought the ticket, she couldn't wait to get there already. The only problem was that her flight wasn't for another four hours. Even worse, she was too afraid to spend the little money that she had on any food. She'd need every penny once she got to London. Despite the fact that she had just downed a milk shake, fries, and an English muffin, she'd kill for something to eat. As she watched a little boy unwrap a chocolate bar, her mouth watered. She couldn't even bear to spare a buck.

Oh, well, I'll eat on the plane, Elizabeth thought. *For twelve hundred bucks I deserve a good meal!* Right then, though, she needed to distract herself from her rumbling stomach and her nervous thoughts. *I'll read,* she told herself, reaching into her backpack for *Pride and Prejudice.* A classic English novel was just what she needed to lose herself in. The hours would pass in no time. Or they would if the chair wasn't so uncomfortable and the airport wasn't so noisy.

Maybe I'll meet my own Mr. Darcy, Elizabeth thought two hours later, smiling wistfully to herself. Someone with opinions and fire that she could spar with . . . but then flirt and fall hopelessly in love with. Yet somehow she had a feeling that even if she did meet someone like that, she wouldn't be interested. Just like she couldn't get interested in even chatting with Nigel. It would take a long, long time before she would feel ready to be with a guy again—before she'd *trust* a guy again. Elizabeth shuddered. She didn't think that the rest of her life would be long enough.

She closed her eyes as she remembered how much she loved Sam's kiss, the feel of his warm, strong hands on her shoulders, her face. She'd been so in love. And she'd been such a damned fool.

At least I caught him and Jessica in the act before I lost my virginity, Elizabeth realized. She couldn't imagine how she would have felt if she'd caught Sam and Jessica together *after* she and Sam had made love.

I've got to stop thinking about this! Elizabeth ordered herself, slamming the book shut in frustration. Was she going to spend the rest of her life having every single thing remind her of Jessica and Sam's treachery? How could something as innocent as reading Jane Austen bring her to the brink of tears?

Of course, she could always think of something else. *Yeah, like how my parents just totally rejected me.* Elizabeth choked back a sob. Who was she kidding, sitting around reading Jane Austen like she didn't have a care in the world? She was about an inch away from totally losing it—forever.

A commotion near the boarding gate made her

look up. An older woman dressed in a leopard-skin coat and dripping with emeralds was having a fit. Elizabeth looked on, fascinated, as a flight attendant removed a miniature schnauzer from underneath the voluminous folds of her fur coat.

"But my Fifi can't travel in the baggage area," the woman shrieked. "She simply must go first-class with me. I really can't have her traveling with all the mutts in steerage."

The flight attendant attempted to calm the woman down as Fifi bared her teeth and snapped at his hands.

"And another thing," the woman continued, her nasal voice screechy and upset. "Fifi requires caviar, not that puppy-chow nonsense you offer in steerage."

Elizabeth could hardly contain herself. She clapped a hand over her mouth to hold back the giggles that were bursting forth. She'd never seen anything as ridiculous in her entire life. The flight attendant led the woman and dog away, Fifi and her owner yapping the entire time. Elizabeth smiled and leaned back in her seat, her eyes suddenly droopy.

When her eyes opened, she straightened up in her chair, disoriented. She wasn't sure how long she'd been asleep, but however long, it wasn't nearly enough. A glance at her watch told her that she'd been out for over an hour, but as far as she was concerned, it felt more like five minutes.

Why did I wake up? Elizabeth wondered grumpily. She stretched her arms over her head and looked around. *That's why,* she thought, eyeing the ten-year-old boy who'd plopped down on the chair next to her, playing with his handheld video game like a madman. She looked at her watch. Her flight would board in a half hour.

A half hour. In thirty minutes she'd be sitting on a plane that would take her to another country.

Nervous, happy, scared, upset, thrilled. Elizabeth felt every emotion a person could possibly feel. But as much as she knew she was doing the right thing, she couldn't help but wish that her parents had given her their blessing.

"They don't even know I'm going," she mumbled to herself. "Me, someone who never even dared cross the street when I was in grade school without getting a permission slip from my mom, is flying off to London without even telling anybody."

"Huh?" the kid next to her said, barely looking up from his game.

She didn't bother replying. Suddenly sad, Elizabeth stood up and lugged her backpack over her shoulder, prepared to head toward the gate for her flight. She walked toward the main concourse, each step harder and harder to take.

"Elizabeth!"

For a moment she thought she'd heard her mother's voice. But that was wishful thinking. It'd be a long time before—

"Elizabeth!" She turned around. "Elizabeth, over here!"

She stopped, her heart racing as she tried to make out a familiar face in the crowd.

But there wasn't one . . . there were two. *Oh my God*. Her mother and her father were running up the walkway toward her.

Ned and Alice Wakefield were in Chicago.

Why?

Chapter Nine

That question was quickly answered. They were there to chew her out. Thoroughly.

"I don't understand how a daughter of mine could behave this way!" Ned Wakefield boomed. He was so angry that his face was turning red. Normally when her father traveled for work, he wore a dark suit with a crisp shirt and tie. Today he wore khakis, a faded polo shirt, and scuffed tennis shoes.

Her mom didn't look much better in her old gardening jeans, streaks of mascara running down her cheeks and her hair droopy and flat.

They must have just dropped whatever they were doing and flown out here, Elizabeth realized, shrinking away from her father. They both looked so crazed, it was a wonder security had even passed them through.

Her mom stood silently by his side, her face twisted into a stern mask. Both of them had been yelling at Elizabeth nonstop for the past five minutes, and they didn't show any signs of letting up soon.

"Are you going to answer me?" her father demanded. "Can you tell me how something like this happened?" His voice got louder with each word, and Elizabeth shrank even farther away from him. "What do you have to say for yourself?"

The truth was that Elizabeth had *nothing* to say. She was completely and totally in shock.

Her parents, who as far as she knew had been home in Sweet Valley when she'd called them, were suddenly in O'Hare Airport. In Chicago, Illinois. What the heck were they doing there? They couldn't possibly have flown into O'Hare to yell at her. Could they? With each outburst of her father and with each of her mother's stern looks and head shakes, it sure seemed that way.

What a fool she'd been. When she'd heard her mom's voice, when she'd seen her parents running toward her, she'd been stupid enough to think that perhaps they'd come all this way to make up with her. To apologize and tell her they loved her. That she must have had a very good reason for ditching Jessica and taking off in the Jeep, and whatever happened, they would listen and understand.

But that wasn't why they were here. Not by a long shot.

Her father shook his head, trying to come up with some new attack against her. People had begun moving away from them, and everyone was staring at them. Elizabeth felt like crawling into a hole.

"Ned," her mom said, facing her husband. "I really think that we should go somewhere a little more private." She laid a hand on his arm and gestured to a grouping of empty seats.

Elizabeth trooped dutifully behind her parents, much too dazed to do anything else. Some part of her brain, however, was registering that her flight would begin boarding in a few minutes and that they were near the departure gate. That gave Elizabeth some comfort. She could calm her parents down, explain her plans, be able to hug and kiss them good-bye, and not miss her plane.

"Well," her father demanded. "I'm waiting."

Elizabeth opened her mouth, then clamped it shut. Where could she possibly begin so that they'd understand?

"Elizabeth," her mom began. "You haven't said two words in the past ten minutes. Don't you think you owe us an explanation? You can begin by telling us why you stranded your sister at the motel and took the Jeep."

Elizabeth blinked back the tears threatening to overtake her. "I—I . . ." She stared down at the dark floor and scuffed the toe of her sneaker against it. "I . . . we . . . we got into a fight."

"We know that already," her dad bit out. "That doesn't excuse what you did."

"This is the kind of behavior we'd expect of your sister, not you, Elizabeth," her mom went on.

Elizabeth's mouth fell open. Did they hear themselves? Did they even realize how crazy that sounded? So if Jessica had stranded Elizabeth in some fleabag motel in the middle of nowhere, that wouldn't require an explanation? That would be just *Jessica being flighty, irresponsible, but lovable old Jess?*

"But it's not fair to criticize Jessica," her father went on. "She's the one lying in a hospital with a broken ankle, waiting for us to get there." Mr. Wakefield shook his head.

So that was why her parents had flown from Sweet Valley to Chicago. Not for Elizabeth. For Jessica. It was always about Jessica.

From now on it's going to be about me, she thought fiercely. After almost twenty years in Jessica's irresponsible shadow, it was about time. "Mom, Dad, I don't mean to sound disrespectful, but I'm going to tell you how I feel," Elizabeth began, suddenly *not* feeling nervous. "I won't tell you what happened with Jessica because that's between her and me. And I doubt she'll tell you either." Or maybe her sister would spin some crazy lie. Whatever. Elizabeth didn't care. *She'd* keep her silence and her dignity. "I think you owe *me* an explanation."

"We owe *you* one?" her father spluttered angrily.

"That's right," Elizabeth said calmly. What she was about to say was long coming, but nothing had ever felt more right. She took a deep breath. "You see, you don't know what happened back in Springfield, but you do know *me*." She paused for a second, realizing how true that statement was, how *right* her argument truly was. "You've known me and Jessica our whole lives, and you know how we've always been. You know that Jessica's always been wild and irresponsible, and you know that *I've* always been hardworking and *responsible*. That should be enough for you."

Elizabeth swallowed back a lump that was forming in her throat. "How many times has Jessica gotten herself into trouble?" she asked as the tears filled her eyes and ran down her cheeks. "When she called you and told you her side of things, why was your first reaction to fly out here to save her and to condemn me for the horrible act of stranding her?"

"Elizabeth, we're not trying to condemn you," her father insisted. "But we want to know the truth of what went on, and nothing you've said is an excuse for why you left your sister all alone and took the Jeep. That Jeep belongs to both of you, and—"

Elizabeth shook her head. "Dad, Jessica deserved being stranded. If she had no insurance card, it's because she's too irresponsible to carry her own things and knows I wouldn't lose it. If she had no money, it's because she's too irresponsible to keep track of what she spends. And if she broke her ankle, it's because she's too irresponsible to watch where she's going!"

"Elizabeth—," her mom began.

But Elizabeth couldn't stop. As the tears fell down her face, she ranted on. "Why didn't you say to yourselves, 'Well, we can trust Elizabeth, but Jess has been in some pretty wild situations before. Elizabeth must have had a good reason for doing what she did.' All you cared about was Jessica!"

Her mom reached out a hand to touch Elizabeth's shoulder. "We didn't know what to think, honey." For a moment her voice softened. "We were just so scared. You're right—you've never done anything like this before. That's why we're trying to get to the bottom of this. You're acting so out of character, and it worries us."

"Oh, Mom." Elizabeth was so hurt, and she was so scared of going so far away, to another country, with no family behind her. She so much wanted things to work out. Was it possible that they could? Hadn't her mom—in her own way— just been apologizing to her? If only they both would really apologize, admit that they were wrong. Elizabeth would meet them halfway.

She turned to her father, but not before a sudden flurry of movement caught her eye. People were lining up at the British Airways gate. Her flight was going to be boarding any minute now. Elizabeth's heart started pounding like a jackhammer. What was going to happen? Was she really going to go to England without her parents' blessing? Or were they going to tell her how sorry they were?

"Dad?" Elizabeth said, her voice a tiny quaver.

Would her father say he was sorry?

"We don't have time for this now, Elizabeth," her father said. "Jessica's waiting. You'll come with us, you'll apologize to her, and we'll deal with your behavior later. We're going to have to spend the night in Chicago, and I want to stop at the visitors' desk and have them go ahead and book a room for us."

Elizabeth stared at her father as if he'd gone stark raving mad. *Maybe I didn't hear him right,* she thought. It was hard to hear anything since her flight was being called and the noise was drowning out everything.

My flight's being called! Elizabeth realized, bolting up. It was now or never. She had to work things out with her parents, she simply had to, or in a matter of moments she would be parted from them for a long, long time.

"Mom, Dad," Elizabeth began. "I have something to tell you. Earlier this year I applied to a semester-abroad program. I've been accepted to the University of London for the fall. And I've decided to go." She raised her ticket so that they could see it. "And now my flight's being called."

"What?" her mom said, staring at her. "Elizabeth, what in the world are you talking about?"

"I just told you, Mom. I've been accepted on a full scholarship, and I'm going. I've made my decision. A semester away from Sweet Valley is exactly what I need."

"I don't care what you've decided," Mr. Wakefield said, hands on hips. "I'm your father, and I've decided that you're coming with us to the hospital and then to the hotel."

They weren't even listening to her. All they seemed to care about was Jessica. Jessica, Jessica, Jessica.

"I don't think you're listening to me," Elizabeth cried, her eyes filling with tears. "I'm not going to the hospital, I'm not going to some stupid Chicago hotel, and I'm sure not going home. I'm going to London!"

Her father grabbed her arm. "You are really pushing the limits of my patience, young lady."

"British Airways flight number two-two-eight-eight is boarding rows twenty-five through thirty. . . ."

Elizabeth yanked her arm away. "In case you weren't paying attention, I'm nineteen now. You can't tell me what I can and cannot do. You're my parents, and I love you, but you don't have a say anymore in how I live my life . . . or where I live it."

She slung her backpack over her shoulder and gripped her ticket. "I'm sorry. I'm sorry we have to part like this. But I'm going to London."

She turned around and squeezed shut her eyes, walking slowly toward the line of people waiting to board. She half expected her father to tackle her, her mom to drag her out to a waiting taxicab . . . but there was nothing except the frantic screams they directed toward her.

"Elizabeth! Come back!" her mom cried.

"Elizabeth Wakefield, come back this instant!" her father yelled.

But Elizabeth didn't. She took a deep breath, handed the ticket to the flight attendant, and boarded the plane.

*　　　*　　　*

Tears were streaming freely down Elizabeth's face as she stepped into the covered corridor that led to the plane. The woman collecting the boarding passes had been too polite to comment on her stricken state, but it seemed like she was the only one. Everyone else that she passed looked at her like she'd grown two heads.

Ordinarily Elizabeth would have been embarrassed, but she was beyond caring. She was much too frightened, hurt, and alone to care about anything else. She wondered if she'd ever be able to care about anything else again. It was hard for her to believe the way her life had unraveled so completely, and she kept replaying the devastated look on her mom's face as she turned her back on her and her father and walked through the gate.

Elizabeth waited in line as the flight attendant directed the person in front of her toward his seat. She choked back a spasm of fear as she looked up and down the aisles of the plane. Was she doing the right thing? She knew that she couldn't have gone back to Sweet Valley with her parents, and she knew that she couldn't have faced Jessica again, but was she in any frame of mind to fly to another country and begin a new life?

A new life with so little to her name?

Fear—cold, hot, and stinging—traveled up Elizabeth's spine. What was she doing? Should she turn around and run after her parents? Make up with them?

No! she told herself resolutely. *They've proved they don't even know who you are. You're just a stereotype to them. A bunch of expectations. You're not real to them. And they've shown that they only care about Jessica. Jessica and her stupid broken ankle!*

You're on your own, Elizabeth. You're on your own, and you'd better get used to it right now.

But you know who you are, girl. And you'll be okay.

So why were the tears coming fast and furious? Elizabeth pulled a tissue out of her pocket and blotted her eyes. She had to get herself under control.

"Elizabeth!"

Elizabeth whipped her head around. She was stunned to hear someone calling her name. Who could possibly know her here?

"Daphne!" She was startled to see the friend she'd made this morning at the diner comfortably ensconced in first class. "What are you doing here? I thought your flight was hours ago."

"It was," Daphne replied. She looked extremely comfortable as she leaned back against the extra-wide plush seats. "But the flight was overbooked, so I agreed to get bumped for a first-class seat! Awesome, huh? I had to hang in the airport, for, like, hours, but I didn't care."

"I can see why," Elizabeth murmured as she took in Daphne's luxurious accommodations. She glanced at the back of the plane, where her own seat was. It looked mighty cramped in comparison. *Yeah, right, like that's my biggest problem.*

"Are you all right?" Daphne asked with a concerned look. "Stupid question—you're obviously not. What happened?" She patted the empty seat next to her. "Sit down and spill."

"It's a really long and ugly story," Elizabeth said quietly as she collapsed on the seat and took the fresh tissue that Daphne was offering. It was much too personal to talk about with a relative stranger, but she was glad to see a familiar face, and she knew that as upset as she was, it would make the long flight easier if she had someone to talk to.

The flight attendant was suddenly standing over her without a smile. "I'm sorry, but you can't sit here, miss. This seat belongs to someone else."

Elizabeth hopped up. "Sorry."

The flight attendant asked Elizabeth for her ticket stub. The woman eyed it, then handed it back. "Your seat is A twenty-nine, on the left of the plane. You can visit with your friend once we're in the air, but right now you need to get to your seat and fasten your seat belt so that we can prepare for takeoff."

Elizabeth smiled at Daphne and headed toward the back of the plane, waiting for people to stow their luggage and take their seats. *I'm in shock,* she thought. *I must be.* She barely felt herself breathing. *Am I really on a plane to London? Did I really catch my sister all over my boyfriend only twenty-four hours ago? Did I really just fight with my parents and majorly disobey them for the first time in my life?*

She had.

Elizabeth thought back to when she'd first applied to the writing program at the University of London. Before she and Sam had hooked up. Before she and Jessica had started fighting nonstop over how much she couldn't stand Sam.

Before any of them had ever taken off on their summer road trip.

Back then, before everything, while she'd filled out the application with hopes and dreams, she'd imagined this moment. Flying to London, anticipating her arrival, wondering what her dorm would look like, who her new friends would be, how she would get around the amazing city of London. But how differently it had all turned out! Instead of her friends and family hugging her good-bye and congratulating her through their tears, she was alone, cut off from her parents. She was headed to London in a wrinkled pair of jeans and a cardigan, practically penniless.

Elizabeth closed her eyes, hoping the line would move soon. Because surely her knees would give out at any minute.

Finally, movement. Elizabeth eyed the seat numbers, grateful that she had a window seat. She could burrow herself in, lean her head against the cool window, and cry her eyes out for the next seven hours—or however long the flight was.

"Excuse me," she said to the guy sitting in the aisle seat of her row. "I'm in there." She pointed to the window seat.

The guy glanced up, and Elizabeth's mouth dropped open. It was Nigel, her savior from the restaurant!

"Well, as you Americans say, it's a small world," Nigel said with a smile.

Elizabeth was too surprised to reply as she stuffed her backpack into the overhead compartment. Nigel got up to let Elizabeth pass through. As she sat down in her seat, Nigel took his seat beside her and buckled himself back in. Elizabeth did the same.

"Should I be flattered that you've been following me around?" Nigel asked, drumming the copy of *Vanity Fair* that rested on his lap. "Obviously my particular brand of British charm proved too much for you after all. Of course, I can't say I'm surprised."

Elizabeth couldn't believe it, but he'd actually made her smile. "I thought your flight was hours ago," she said. The truth was that she did think Nigel was charming, but she could no more respond to his witty banter than she could fly across the ocean without the plane.

"I didn't have a ticket, actually," Nigel said, placing his book in the seat pocket. "I was trying for standby, and this is the flight I got."

"Well . . . it's nice to see a friendly face." Elizabeth smiled wanly. Now that she was on the plane, strapped in and ready to go, all she wanted to do was lean back and not think for the next hundred hours.

Nice try. No matter how she tried to clear her mind, she couldn't stop seeing her parents' faces, full of confusion and disappointment. When was the last time she saw her parents look at her with disappointment in their faces? Maybe never.

Oh, Mom, oh, Dad, how could you treat me that way? She bit her lip to keep herself from crying, but it wasn't any use. She could feel the hot tears start to prick her eyelids. She choked back a sob and rummaged in her pocket for the tissues that Daphne had given her moments before. Somehow she'd managed to lose them in that short time.

Elizabeth didn't know why something as stupid as losing some tissues should seem so monumental, but it did. It was the last straw. She hunted for them for a few seconds, then gave up and burst into tears.

Nigel couldn't help but notice. "I'm sorry to pry, but could I help?"

Elizabeth couldn't answer. She buried her head in her hands and sobbed uncontrollably. Some part of her brain dimly registered that Nigel was pressing a white linen handkerchief in her hands and that he was discreetly returning to his book. Elizabeth accepted the hankie gratefully and proceeded to drown it with her tears.

How could they have rejected me like that? she wept. She simply couldn't believe that all the love her parents had showered on her over the years had disappeared overnight. Deep inside she supposed that her parents still loved her, but they had still betrayed her. When the chips were down, they'd taken Jessica's side. Jessica, who'd committed an unforgivable act against her own twin sister. Jessica, who'd always been irresponsible and selfish. Her parents had chosen Jessica.

The tears kept flowing as scenes from her childhood flashed before her. Elizabeth remembered the look on her parents' face when she and Jessica had first brought home Prince Albert, their dog.

She remembered shopping for school clothes with her mom. Her father helping her with her math homework. Then the picture shifted slightly, and she remembered the time that Jessica had impersonated her and emptied Elizabeth's bank account. She'd been so angry at first! Looking back at it now, she couldn't believe that she'd ever been upset by something so trivial.

She couldn't seem to stop the memories from bombarding her. Her heart broke all over again as she remembered the time that she'd lain in a hospital bed after a motorcycle accident and Jessica had kept a prayer vigil by her bed. In the depths of her soul Elizabeth knew that she owed her recovery to Jessica's devotion.

Oh, Jess, she thought, sobbing. *How could you have done what you did to me? We had such an incredible bond. How could you have hurt me so badly? How, how?*

"If you need to talk," Nigel said, breaking in on her thoughts, "I'm a good listener, and I'm free for the next nine hours or so."

"Thank you," Elizabeth managed to say between sobs. She was touched by his kindness, but she really didn't think that she could share her story with anyone.

"Maybe you should try and get some sleep," Nigel continued after a moment. "I can wake you up when the food comes."

"That's okay." Elizabeth smiled weakly. "I'm sorry you have such a mess for a seat partner. I've just . . . been through a lot," she finished.

"Well, let's at least make you comfortable, shall we?" Nigel said as he ripped open the plastic wrapper covering the complimentary blanket. He wrapped the blanket around Elizabeth and then tucked a puffy white pillow tenderly under her head.

His kindness only made Elizabeth feel worse. There was something pathetically sad about the fact that total strangers were being so sweet while her own family had treated her so horribly.

Elizabeth would normally pay attention to the flight attendant standing in the front of the plane, going over the safety regulations, but tonight she could barely manage to pay attention to the fact that the plane had seemed to rumble to life.

Soon the flight attendants had finished their spiels, and the plane pulled away from the gate. Then the plane began to taxi down the runway. Fast. Very fast. Elizabeth's teary eyes widened as there was a slight bump, the wings shuddered, and then the plane lifted smoothly into the sky like a great bird. Elizabeth craned her neck to catch the last glimpse of the Chicago skyline, twinkling beneath her like a mass of silvery stars.

"Good-bye," she whispered to herself. "Good-bye, Sweet Valley. Good-bye, everyone."

She wiped away some fresh tears with Nigel's sodden handkerchief and snuggled into the blanket that he'd tucked around her. She was surprised to find herself dozing off. Sure, she was exhausted, but she'd figured that her misery would keep her up all night.

Good-bye, good-bye, floated through Elizabeth's mind like a sad little lullaby as she drifted off to sleep.

Chapter
Ten

Elizabeth woke with a start, unsure of where she was. The lights were out on board, and she was totally disoriented for a second. It took the throbbing hum of the engines and a crick in her neck to remind her of where she was, and as soon as she knew, the pain came back, even sharper than it had been before.

I've got to stop mourning, Elizabeth thought as she rearranged the blanket that she'd kicked off in her sleep. *I've got to get ahold of myself.* She knew that if she kept giving way to her feelings, she'd go crazy. While she was sure that she'd be in pain, deep pain, for a long, long, time, she had to find a more constructive way to deal with her feelings.

If I could just look at this as an adventure, she reflected as she stretched her cramped legs out in the small space in front of her. After all, as bad as things were, there were *some* things to look forward to. She was going to one of the world's great capitals, a historic and beautiful city. Not only that, but she was going to be involved in what promised to be a highly challenging and fascinating creative-writing program.

Who knows—maybe I could even meet a cutie on campus like Nigel, Elizabeth thought as she studied his sleeping profile. If Nigel was anything to go by, British men were awfully nice.

Unfortunately, just thinking about having a relationship was enough to bring the tears back. *Stop it!* Elizabeth chided herself. She was supposed to be making herself feel better, not worse.

Maybe I just need a little company to help me take my mind off things, Elizabeth mused. It looked like Nigel was out, but what about Daphne? She got up, climbed over his legs, and began walking unsteadily toward first class.

As she navigated her way through the cabin, she poked her head into the tiny galley kitchen, where the flight attendants were busy loading what looked like TV dinners into the microwave. Elizabeth knew that airplane food was terrible, but she was so hungry that her mouth watered at the sight of the little trays.

"Dinner will be in about half an hour," one of the attendants said to Elizabeth.

Elizabeth nodded and continued up the aisle. She was surprised by how small everything was. There was hardly any legroom, and people were stuffed into their seats like sardines in a can. In a way Elizabeth was glad to know it wasn't only her row that was tiny. *Next time I'll fly first-class*, she thought with a smile. She couldn't even imagine how much a first-class, last minute flight cost. Ten thousand dollars, maybe.

Elizabeth found Daphne's silky brown head and knelt beside her seat. "Hi," she whispered, just in case Daphne was sleeping.

But Daphne turned around with a grin. "Hey, yourself." Daphne removed her earphones, which were plugged into her own personal video console. "How are you doing?" She looked concerned. "Feeling any better?"

"A little," Elizabeth admitted. She was struck once again by how kind mere acquaintances were being. "It's pretty uncomfortable back there, though." She grinned. "So I'd thought I'd slum with you for a while. Hey, where's your seat mate?" Elizabeth plopped down into the empty, wide, plush chair next to Daphne with a sigh.

"I think she's stretching her legs and walking around the cabin," Daphne explained. "So, hang out here till she comes back. Oh, I almost forgot," she added, reaching into the seat pocket in front of her and taking out several glossy books. "I've got some great guidebooks on London. Do you know the city at all?"

"I'm clueless," Elizabeth admitted, reaching eagerly for a book. "I guess I should have bought some guides in the bookshop at the airport, but I was so preoccupied." She flipped through one of the books. "I can't believe I'm actually going to see Big Ben in person," she said as she looked at a large photograph of the famous clock tower.

Daphne nodded. "I could be wrong, but I think the University of London isn't far from there. Let me pull it up on my laptop."

Elizabeth grinned. "That would be great. Thanks, Daphne." She settled back against the soft blue plush and waited for Daphne's laptop to boot up. Now that she was determined to make the best of things, she was feeling a little bit curious and excited about what awaited her in England.

Daphne typed and clicked, and moments later a map of London appeared on her screen. "Yup, I was right," she said. "I mean, it's not across the street or anything—the college is a little closer to Trafalgar Square—but you'll probably pass Big Ben every day."

"A little different than walking by the palm trees and bleached-blond, cell-phone-carrying skaters at Sweet Valley University, I guess," Elizabeth joked.

Daphne clicked on a link, and Big Ben itself appeared on the screen. "London's amazing!" she said, looking from the screen to Elizabeth and back. "My boyfriend and I went there for six weeks before

113

senior year. We had the best time—there's really something for everyone. They've got the best theater in the world, an awesome music scene, great clubs, the best shopping for clothes and cool shoes. Anything you want, any style, any food, any anything, you can get there. After that trip I realized how silly I was never to have applied for a semester-abroad program. You are so lucky, Elizabeth. Everything you could possibly want, you'll have in London."

Except my family. The thought came out of nowhere, and Elizabeth found herself blinking back tears. *When will I feel better?* she asked herself. She turned away slightly so that Daphne wouldn't see the brightness in her eyes. It was crazy that her upbeat mood could have evaporated so quickly. She'd been perfectly content to surf the Web with Daphne, looking for interesting sights, and then *wham!*

What was it she had seen on *Oprah* once? That you needed to give yourself time to grieve before you could move on. She knew, of course, that her life hadn't been that tragic—no one had actually died. But she was still grieving, in a sense—grieving over what might have been with Sam, grieving over the nasty riff she and Jessica had had, grieving over the fact that she was growing up and moving away from her family on such unpleasant terms.

Elizabeth made a visible effort to focus on what Daphne was saying. She swallowed the giant lump in her throat and turned back to the computer.

"I mean, if you're a student, London is like an open city," Daphne continued enthusiastically. "You can get into the museums for free, you can stay at youth hostels for practically nothing, and you can even get theater tickets at a discount."

"It does sound great," Elizabeth agreed as she flipped through the guidebook.

"You're gonna love it," Daphne insisted. "I mean, for someone like you, who's a writer, it's got to be the most interesting city on the planet. Did you know that you can go to the British Library reading room and see original manuscripts by Milton?"

"You're kidding!" Elizabeth was impressed in spite of herself. *If I just get involved in things, then I won't be able to focus on how much pain I'm in,* she told herself firmly.

"Really. Look, I'm not going to be that busy for the first few days—I can probably show you." Daphne ripped a piece of paper out of one of the flight magazines and scribbled an address on it. "That's the youth hostel where I'm staying. Once you get settled, you should look me up."

"I'd love to," Elizabeth said sincerely as she glanced at the address. "Don't look at me like I'm an idiot, by the way, but what's a youth hostel?"

"They're like glorified dorm rooms," Daphne explained. "You have to be a student to stay in them, and they're hardly luxury accommodations, but they make life pretty easy. They're pretty cheap, like ten or twenty dollars a night."

"Sounds good," Elizabeth said as she tucked the slip of paper in her back pocket. "So what are you planning to do once you get settled?"

"It depends on what my boyfriend and I decide on," Daphne said, and Elizabeth felt a fresh shaft of pain pierce her soul.

How much fun would London have been with Sam by her side? They could have gone to the British Library or whatever it was called. They could have gone to the theater together.

Who was she kidding? Sam checking out Milton manuscripts at a museum? Sam at the theater? He hated that stuff. Sam was strictly beer and dartboards and Cheez Doodles and video games and—

And so what the heck were you doing with him? she asked herself. Could they have had *less* in common? Suddenly she wasn't feeling as sad as she'd been moments ago. Suddenly she felt free. Free to see and do what she wanted in London.

On second thought, that sounded pretty lonely. . . .

Guess I'll be tagging along after Daphne or else doing those things alone, Elizabeth realized with a sigh. She knew she should be grateful that she was being given so many wonderful opportunities, but she just couldn't stop hurting.

"First we're gonna try to get jobs, make a few bucks before we travel." Daphne signed off the Internet and shut down her laptop.

"But I thought you were taking the year off," Elizabeth said in surprise.

"Hey, I don't mean I'm going to go the corporate route," Daphne explained with a laugh. "Maybe serving pints in a pub or working in the back of a restaurant or becoming a maid. Those are the only jobs you can get over there without working papers anyway."

Elizabeth nodded, but a photo in the guidebook, a picture of the famous crown jewels, caught her attention. Even on paper the magnificence of the rubies and diamonds was breathtaking. And to think she would be able to see them with her own eyes in mere hours if she chose! How cool was that?

A flight attendant hovered over Elizabeth in the aisle. "I'm sorry, miss," the woman said, "but you'll have to return to your own seat for the meal service. Also, if you're not a holder of a British passport, you'll need to fill out a customs form to hand in at the customs counter in the airport. You'll receive the form at your seat along with your meal." The flight attendant smiled and moved off down the aisle.

"Why do I get the feeling that your meal is going to be, like, a million times better than mine?" Elizabeth joked. She really didn't care that much about the food one way or another, just as long as she got something to eat. She was starving and broke.

"You're right about that one," Daphne said, waving a fancy-looking menu at Elizabeth. "Look, filet mignon, lobster, the works."

Elizabeth immediately thought back to the last time she'd eaten lobster. Of course it had been with Sam, and of course Sam hadn't even enjoyed it. As far as he was concerned, if it didn't come in a fast-food wrapper, it wasn't worth eating.

I'm better off without him, she told herself, trying to convince herself that going to a fancy restaurant with someone like Nigel would be more fun than eating french fries in a parking lot with Sam, but it didn't work.

You were in love with the guy yesterday, she reminded herself. *Give yourself a break, Liz. You're allowed to have a broken heart.*

"Hey," Daphne said, waving a hand in front of her face. "You look like you've seen a ghost or something."

"Sorry." Elizabeth offered a small smile. "I'm just really wiped out. I guess I should be getting back."

"See you later," Daphne said.

Elizabeth reluctantly—very reluctantly—got up from the wide, plush seat just in time to see the flight attendant place a very elegant looking tray in front of

Daphne. Elizabeth caught a glimpse of real linen napkins and a silver bud vase with a dark red rose.

"Hey," Daphne called out to Elizabeth.

Elizabeth turned around.

Daphne threw her a little package wrapped in gold foil. "You can have my after-dinner mint, okay?"

Elizabeth grinned, then laughed. "Thanks." She unwrapped the mint and popped it in her mouth as she made her way back to her seat.

She was glad she'd stopped to talk to Daphne; their conversation had helped cheer her up—at least, to the extent that she was able to get excited about all the great stuff there was to see and do in London.

I learned something just now, Elizabeth realized as she sucked thoughtfully on the mint. *I learned that my school is near Big Ben, I learned that I can get theater tickets at a discount, I learned about youth hostels, and I learned that I can control my thoughts and not think about what happened for about, say, ten minutes out of every hour.*

Somehow she'd have to learn to deal with the other fifty minutes.

"I hate to think what kind of animal this came from." Nigel made a face as he cut into his entrée.

"Uh, I think it's supposed to be poultry," Elizabeth said dubiously. She was glad that she'd selected the pasta offering.

"In that case, if you don't mind a seriously bad pun, this poultry is foul." Nigel smiled at her. "But seriously, do you think it could possibly be buzzard?"

Elizabeth laughed at the expression on his face. She hated to admit it, but as hungry as she was, the food tasted delicious. Besides, after eating at roadside motels for days, she was hardly in a mood to be critical.

"Oh, I don't know," she said, swallowing a forkful of linguine. "Mine's not that bad. It kind of reminds me of the pasta my brother, Steven, and my sister made when we were first learning how to cook. . . ." She trailed off, amazed that something so trivial could have the power to make her so sad at the drop of a hat.

"There you go again," Nigel said, studying her closely. "Where do you disappear to when you get that look on your face?"

Elizabeth toyed with her food and didn't answer for a moment. He was too perceptive, and she was unsure of what to say.

"Is that a polite way of telling me to mind my own business?" he asked softly.

Elizabeth shook her head. "No. Nigel, I'm sorry if I've been distant and not too friendly. I mean, you've been really, really nice. It's just that I've had a hard time lately, that's all." She looked at him with a sad smile.

"I see." Nigel pushed aside his tray. "Well," he said, turning to her with a quirky grin. "You're awfully mysterious. Who are you now, and who were you before?"

"Casablanca!" Elizabeth exclaimed. She'd recognized the Humphrey Bogart lines immediately.

"Ah." Nigel nodded. "I see you're up on your classic films. Can I take it that you're an old-movie buff like myself?"

"Not really." Elizabeth grinned. "But I had an old boyfriend who'd practically memorized every film ever made between 1930 and 1945." It was true—Tom Watts had adored the great old movies from Hollywood's golden era.

"Sounds like a guy of rare good taste." Nigel tried a bite of the hard chocolate brownie that was tonight's dessert.

"I guess he was," Elizabeth murmured absently, aware that she wasn't really listening to Nigel anymore. She hated being rude, especially when she'd opened up about herself, just a little, moments ago. But she couldn't help it. Suddenly she was thinking about Tom Watts and their relationship.

There was a time, right after they'd broken up, when Elizabeth was in so much agony that she could barely get through the day, but now things were different. Time had blunted the sharp edge of her misery, and she could remember the good things about Tom—and the bad—without wanting to burst into tears.

When had that happened? Elizabeth couldn't pinpoint the moment that heartbreak had changed to a kind of indifference. But it had. If, in the first tumultuous months after their breakup, someone had told her that there would come a time when she wouldn't care about Tom anymore, well, she just wouldn't have believed them.

I guess if I could get over Tom, then I can get over this too, Elizabeth thought, a small ray of hope blossoming inside her. *It's just going to be tough, that's all.*

Somehow the thought made Elizabeth feel better. She'd been through bad things before and survived; she would again. She just had to focus on the positive. She needed to think about the good things that were going to happen to her—not the bad things that already had.

"So," Nigel said, breaking into her thoughts. "May I ask what you're going to be doing on my side of the pond? I don't mean to pry, but I'm quite curious as to why a beautiful American is descending on London."

Elizabeth blushed. She had a very hard time believing she looked anything resembling *attractive* with her puffy eyes and red nose. "School. I've won a scholarship for a writing program for the fall semester." Elizabeth smiled. "Maybe you've heard of it? It's at the University of London.

"Maybe I've heard of it?" Nigel's mouth hung open. "Are you serious? It's incredibly prestigious. I must say I feel like a bit of a fool."

"Why?" Elizabeth was baffled. She smiled at the flight attendant as the woman cleared her tray away. "Why do you feel like a fool?"

"Well, back when we were at the airport, I was blathering all about myself and Oxford." Nigel looked shamefaced. "You never said that you were a writer too. Clearly you weren't interested in talking, and there I was, going on and on."

Elizabeth smiled. "It's not that I wasn't interested in talking, just that I had my mind on other things." She thought back to her sojourn in the airport and how confused she had been. Well, she wasn't confused any longer. She knew what she was going to do. She was on her way to London. "Forgive me for being rude?"

"No apology necessary," Nigel said with a smile.

Elizabeth smiled back and tucked the blanket back around her. "So, what do you know about the University of London? I have to admit that I don't know much at all. All I have is the acceptance letter."

"Then you'll be glad to hear it has one of the

best writing programs in the United Kingdom," Nigel said. "They have some extraordinary visiting lecturers." He rattled off a list of some very distinguished writers. "I wish some of them would lecture at Oxford."

"Well, Oxford isn't exactly Backwater U," Elizabeth said with a grin. "I'd say you were doing pretty okay."

"Oxford is Oxford, yes, but it's stuffy. As you Americans would say, 'totally' stuffy."

Elizabeth laughed, feeling herself relax.

"But I must say I envy you," Nigel continued. "I had a friend who was in your program, and he loved it. Aside from everything else, you're smack in the heart of London instead of rusticating in the country."

"You had a friend there?" Elizabeth asked, her eyes wide. "So maybe you heard something about the dorm rooms?" The idea of having her own room to decorate was appealing. She'd had her own room in the off-campus house that she'd shared with Jessica, Neil, and Sam, but still, sharing a house meant being forced to deal with other people's tastes and bad habits. Not that Elizabeth was Miss Neat, but—okay, she was. But was that so terrible? Like there was something wrong with her just because she liked clean clothes, a kitchen table free of ketchup blobs, and a shower that wasn't lined with mildew.

"The dorms are great," Nigel said. "Forgive me for saying this, but they're not like the ugly, plain, square boxes you Americans are forced to live in in your universities. At the University of London your room will be in a building that looks like an old castle, with winding stone steps."

"Sounds amazing," Elizabeth murmured. She was feeling tired again, and she was having a hard time keeping her eyes open, but she was feeling something else too. Relief. She could just tell that everything was going to work out. She'd touch down in England, take the train to London, find the university, and spend the semester writing a masterpiece. "It sounds just amazing," she repeated sleepily.

"I'm worn out too," Nigel said as he reached up and turned out the dome light. "Let's get some sleep."

"G'night," Elizabeth mumbled. She closed her eyes and allowed the thrumming of the plane's engines to lull her to sleep.

Chapter Eleven

Elizabeth woke up with a jolt. Her back was aching, her legs were so cramped that she didn't know if she'd ever be able to unbend them, and she was dying of thirst.

"Good morning," Nigel said with a smile.

"Are we there yet?" Elizabeth groaned. She was pretty certain she smelled, and her hair was so tangled that she wondered if it made more sense to cut it off at the first salon she passed than to try and comb it.

The pilot answered her before Nigel could. "Good morning, ladies and gentlemen. We've begun our descent into London's Heathrow International Airport, so you'll need to fasten your seat belts. Flight crew, prepare for cross-check. We will be landing in a few minutes."

Elizabeth's eyes widened, and her stomach felt

as wobbly as her legs. They'd be landing in minutes! In minutes she'd be in England!

She had made sure her passport, her customs form, and the acceptance letter were within easy reach in her backpack. Now she buckled her seat belt and leaned forward to look out the window. It was impossible to see what England really looked like, though, because a fine mist of rain obscured the view.

I'm really here, Elizabeth thought with a lump in her throat. *England!*

Fortunately, there was too much else going on for her to give way to nerves. The plane landed with a bump, and after taxiing for fifteen minutes the aircraft came to a stop, and the seat-belt sign was turned off. Suddenly people jumped out of their seats as if the craft were on fire.

Elizabeth licked her lips and smoothed down her hair as she waited in her seat. Next to her Nigel was gathering his magazines, and she thought she saw him discreetly pop a breath mint into his mouth. Passengers crowded into the aisles, pulling luggage from the overhead compartments. Having a seat in the back meant being the last group off the plane. Finally, movement. The mass of travelers shuffled forward, and Elizabeth squeezed out of her seat, grabbed her backpack, and followed the crowd ahead.

Where did Nigel disappear to? Elizabeth wondered, looking around frantically. Hadn't he been right behind her? She craned her neck and tried to look past the people who were pushing her forward, but she couldn't see him anywhere. She'd lost him in a matter of moments, and she didn't see Daphne anywhere.

Okay, don't stress, Elizabeth told herself in a poor attempt at a pep talk. *You'll hook up with them in the airport.*

Elizabeth walked out of the aircraft and down a long corridor. She hoisted her backpack on her shoulders and pulled the skimpy cardigan that she was wearing more tightly around herself.

Where to now? she wondered as she followed the crowd out of the gate and into the rush of people. It seemed like everyone else there had someone to meet them. She looked for Nigel and Daphne, hoping she'd spot them, but no such luck.

Elizabeth had no idea where to go next. She stopped, aware of people having to walk around her. Men, women, children, people of all races and ages and sizes and accents, headed in all directions, loudspeakers were making announcements, travelers rushed by pushing carts laden with suitcases, and everyone but her looked like they knew what they were doing.

It was more than enough to bring back the overwhelming loneliness that she'd felt back in Chicago. Elizabeth took a deep breath. She'd just follow the signs. Even though she was in a foreign country, at least they spoke English.

Thank goodness I didn't apply to a school in Italy, Elizabeth thought wryly as she followed the arrows to the baggage claim. She recognized several people from her flight heading off in the same general direction, and she followed them as quickly as she could through the long hallway and down the escalator. At the baggage claim Elizabeth saw three revolving carousels overflowing with various suitcases and bags. Neither Nigel nor Daphne was in sight, but thankfully her duffel was. She had to admit, the bag looked pretty pathetic there with all the nice suitcases.

Okay, first hurdle successfully completed, Elizabeth thought as she dragged the duffel toward the exit. Although she'd been worried that she had only the clothes she'd packed for the road trip, she couldn't help feeling glad now that she'd traveled so light. Once her stipend kicked in, she'd be able to pick up some cute outfits, maybe even at Harrods, the famous London department store. She should be grateful she didn't have to lug around some monster of a suitcase.

The next thing that she had to clear was

immigration. Elizabeth followed the signs to the correct line for non-British citizens, holding on to her passport with an iron grip. Her eyes were so bleary that she could barely see five feet in front of her, and all she could think about was crawling into the new bed that would be awaiting her in her dorm room.

"Next," the immigration officer called. Elizabeth nearly tripped over her own feet as she stumbled forward and handed the man her passport.

"Purpose of your visit?" The immigration officer had what Elizabeth believed to be a cockney accent . . . he sounded like one of the characters from *EastEnders,* a British soap she'd watched on public television.

"I'll be attending the University of London," Elizabeth said.

The man studied her passport. "Do you have proof of acceptance from the university?"

Elizabeth pulled out her acceptance letter and handed it to the officer.

The man flicked his eyes over the letter and handed it back to her without a word. He stamped her passport and gave that back to her too.

The exit signs ahead alerted Elizabeth to have her customs form ready to hand in at the door. Elizabeth retrieved it from her backpack, showed her passport to the woman at the door, and then finally entered the main terminal at Heathrow Airport.

If she'd been overwhelmed when she'd gotten off the plane into the hallways leading to customs, it was nothing compared to being set free in a major international airport like Heathrow. It wasn't that it was *so* different from O'Hare International Airport or the Los Angeles airport, but knowing that it was all the way across the Atlantic made Elizabeth very aware of being in a different country. She caught fragments of English accents as people hurried by.

Now that she was through immigration and had her luggage, the only thing left to do was to hail a cab and show up at the school. *That's if I can manage to find one,* Elizabeth thought as she tried to find the street exit. It seemed like there were signs for everything except for where to get a taxi. She looked around for a few moments before giving up in defeat.

Maybe I should just ask someone. Elizabeth glanced around, trying to find a friendly-looking face in the crowd. She caught the eye of a pleasant-faced older woman.

Elizabeth pasted a smile on her face—she was so tired that it was a major effort—and dragged her duffel over to the woman. "Excuse me," Elizabeth said politely. "Could you tell me where I could get a taxi?"

The woman smiled at her, but as the seconds ticked by, it was clear that she wasn't going to respond.

"Excuse me," Elizabeth said a little bit more loudly. Was it possible the woman simply hadn't heard her?

The woman smiled and shook her head at Elizabeth. "No speaka da English." She spread her hands in a gesture of regret.

Great. Elizabeth smiled feebly. So much for that.

"Might I be of assistance?" An older man in a bowler hat tapped Elizabeth on the shoulder.

Elizabeth wheeled around in surprise. She couldn't help smiling at the man's appearance. He looked exactly like an idealized version of an English gentleman, complete with walking stick. "I hope so," Elizabeth said, with genuine relief. "I can't seem to find a taxi. I need to get into London."

"A taxi?" The man cocked a bushy white eyebrow. "Unless you've got pounds to spare, a taxi from Heathrow to London would cost the earth. You're best off going by way of the underground, the tube."

"The tube?" Visions of being shot through some kind of steel cylinder flashed through Elizabeth's mind.

"I think you Americans call it the subway. Over there." The man pointed with his walking stick. Elizabeth saw people hurrying toward what looked like a wall of elevators. She smiled at the gentleman again, then headed over. When the giant doors slid open, Elizabeth entered with everyone else. She realized she was entering the airport's own version of a subway, to get people from terminal to terminal. She noted the stop for the tubes was the next stop and got out when the doors slid back open.

Signs for the underground were everywhere, and Elizabeth headed down a steep flight of stairs. She could hear the roar of trains. She marched over to the ticket window and took out her letter from the university.

"I'd like a ticket to the stop nearest this school, please," she told the ticket agent, handing over the letter. "I think it's near Big Ben."

The woman nodded and slid back the letter. Elizabeth replaced it in her backpack and pulled out a five-dollar bill. Surely it couldn't cost more than that?

"You want the Westminster Street station," the woman behind the counter said. "But you can't get there with U.S. dollars."

"Why not?" Elizabeth asked, baffled.

"Because you're in England, miss," the woman

said slowly, as if Elizabeth were an idiot. "You'll need to exchange your dollars for British pounds."

Of course! Elizabeth thought, her face flaming. How could she have been so stupid to think that she could use American money over here? She felt like such a dummy.

"You can change your money at the booths upstairs," the woman informed her.

Elizabeth nodded wearily and proceeded back up the stairs. This time she really noticed the way her duffel banged her legs, but she tried to reassure herself that it still wouldn't be that long before she was snugly tucked into her new bed in her new dorm room in her new university. *Just a temporary setback, that's all,* she told herself. Luckily the currency-exchange booths were plentiful, and she walked over as quickly as she could.

"I'd like to exchange my U.S. dollars for English pounds, please." Elizabeth handed over her money and even dug into the pockets of her jeans for every last bit of change that she had.

"That's twelve pounds, thirty pence," the woman said with brisk efficiency as she pushed a pile—a very small pile—of British money at Elizabeth. It was all different colors and shapes and looked nothing like American bills.

Elizabeth was shocked at just how little of it there was. Somehow twenty-five dollars felt like a lot more than twelve pounds. She felt uncomfortably vulnerable as she tucked the money away in her wallet.

No need to stress, she told herself, trying to calm down. *Everything's been taken care of, and now you're just a few subway stops—sorry,* tube *stops—away from a cozy dorm room.* Elizabeth decided that once she was settled in and had a nap, she could take care of sorting out her financial stipend.

So stop worrying! She gave herself a mental shake. *Twelve pounds is probably more than enough to last until then!*

It had to be. Because it was all Elizabeth had at the moment.

Elizabeth closed her eyes for a second and leaned back against the deliciously soft fabric of the tube seat. She was shocked by how different the British subway system was from the subways that she'd taken in America.

The tube was more like a fancy train than a subway. Instead of metal seats and walls covered in graffiti, there was comfortable upholstery and attractive advertising posters. Of course the price was different too. Elizabeth had been stunned to see a quarter of her money eaten up in train fare, but there was nothing she could do about that.

I've done it, Elizabeth thought as the train rattled through the tunnel. *I'm on my way!*

She felt a wave of exhaustion wash over her. It was ten-thirty in the morning. But in Chicago time and California time, it was . . . Elizabeth was so tired, she couldn't think. All she knew was that she'd taken a 7:30 P.M. flight, and it was now 10:30 A.M., but there was a major time difference in there too somewhere.

Elizabeth realized she couldn't think because she was suffering from the famous jet lag—that wonderful combination of time changes and not enough sleep and excitement and nerves. She was so tired. But she was afraid that if she closed her eyes, she'd fall asleep and miss her stop. Westminster was called out, and Elizabeth jerked upright. She'd practically nodded off as it was.

The train rattled to a stop. Elizabeth jumped up and nearly tripped over several of her fellow passengers as she grabbed her duffel and raced onto the platform. She followed everyone up the stairs, where doors marked Exit were just a few feet away now. All she had to do was push through them, and she'd be in London.

Elizabeth's lips split into a smile, and she ran toward the doors, her duffel hitting her legs. She pushed through and felt her heart soar.

London.

Elizabeth stood stock-still. She'd never seen anything like it before. It was simply and completely stunning, even when viewed through the gentle rain that misted the horizon.

I can't believe I'm really here, she thought as she drank in the magnificent sight of the Houses of Parliament. They shimmered in their golden glory, serene over the glistening expanse of water, which Elizabeth knew must be the Thames River. It was a sight that she recalled from many paintings and photographs, but nothing could have prepared her for the reality. Elizabeth dimly recalled that when the Houses of Parliament were built, they were the world's largest buildings. No doubt there were bigger ones around now, but if so, Elizabeth had never seen them.

Her heart beat faster as she realized just how exciting her semester was going to be. She knew that her broken heart would be with her for a long, long time, but she also knew that her new surroundings would go a long way toward helping her forget.

I better get a move on, she thought, tearing her eyes away from the awesome spectacle of Parliament. Maybe after a good nap she'd feel up to exploring her new city.

Elizabeth took out her acceptance letter from the university and glanced at the address. According to what the woman at the tube station had told her, the school should be just a few blocks away.

I should have bought a map, Elizabeth realized.

And why did I give Daphne back her guidebook? How she wished she had it now. *Stop worrying,* she told herself. The school couldn't be far and certainly would be known to any Londoner. She'd just have to ask for directions.

"Excuse me." Elizabeth hailed a young man who was striding in the opposite direction. "Can you tell me where, Glous—um . . . Gloust—" The street's name escaped her, and she looked down at the letter again. She wasn't sure how to pronounce it.

"Gloucester Place?" the guy said. "That's about a fifteen-minute walk from here." He pointed in the opposite direction. "You want to walk down the embankment as far as possible, and you'll see signs from there."

"Thank you," Elizabeth said as she turned in the direction that he indicated.

Fifteen minutes sounded like more than a couple of blocks, especially to a Californian like herself who was more at home on the highway than on a sidewalk. She wondered why the woman at the tube stop hadn't suggested a closer station. *Oh, well, I'll be there soon enough,* she reminded herself, her excitement growing.

I'm walking down a London street. Me, Elizabeth Wakefield.

Suddenly, despite her jet lag, despite her lack of money, she felt like skipping.

Chapter Twelve

This doesn't look like a university, Elizabeth thought, frowning as she looked at the exquisite Georgian town house. *But this is 37 Gloucester Place.* She studied the now wrinkled acceptance letter in confusion.

The house didn't look anything like the pictures that Elizabeth had seen in the university prospectus or on the Web. *I mean, I know the camera lies,* she thought, eyeing the house, *but not this much!* Something was definitely screwy. Well, she wouldn't figure out what was going on if she didn't knock on the door. Maybe this was some kind of annex. Maybe this was where they processed visiting scholars.

Maybe this is my dorm, Elizabeth thought, her heart quickening. If so, it was just about the fanciest dorm on the planet.

No, it can't be the dorm, Elizabeth realized.

Nigel had told her that the dorms were in a building that resembled an old castle. But perhaps there were dorms he didn't know about?

Elizabeth took a deep breath and walked up the stone steps, careful not to disturb the gorgeous flowerpots that flanked the entryway. She raised the brass knocker and barely had to tap the door before it was whisked open by a maid straight out of a 1940s movie, complete with a white apron and cap.

Okay, I'm definitely in the wrong place, Elizabeth realized with a sinking feeling in her stomach. Maybe, just *maybe* the university would have a few exclusive residences for the foreign students, but even in her wildest dreams Elizabeth never imagined that they would come with maid service.

"May I help you?" the maid asked.

"I—I hope so," Elizabeth stammered, suddenly acutely aware of how unkempt she must appear. She reached up a hand to smooth her hair. But without a comb and a mirror it was a hopeless job. "I seem to be in the wrong place," she said with a nervous laugh. "Here." She thrust her letter at the maid. "But I *am* at the right address, aren't I?"

"Heavens, no," the maid exclaimed as she bent her head over the letter. "This is Gloucester Place. You want Gloucester *Road*."

Elizabeth shook her head in dismay. How could she have made such a foolish mistake? Well, actually, she knew how. Take an exhausted, overwrought girl, throw in some jet lag for good measure, and add a touch of disorientation at being plunked down in a foreign city, and you had a perfect recipe for disaster. Elizabeth was surprised that nothing worse had happened. After all, she could have overslept her stop, or lost her wallet, or any one of a thousand things.

"Okay," she said, trying not to sound too discouraged. "Could you tell me how to get to Gloucester *Road?*"

"That's quite a walk, especially carrying that bag," the maid said. "It's about a half-hour walk in that direction," she added, pointing toward where Elizabeth had just come from.

"That's all right," Elizabeth replied with more confidence than she felt. She was afraid to spend any more money on the tube. Unfortunately, the gentle mist had turned into genuine drizzle, and Elizabeth was getting wet.

"Head back toward Parliament and then on to Trafalgar Square," the woman said. "You'll be able to see the university from a few blocks away."

"Thank you," Elizabeth said, with the absurd feeling that she should curtsy. She squashed it and hefted her bag as she started off down the street.

Elizabeth tried to be positive as she hobbled along, but she was having a hard time keeping her spirits up. Ordinarily she wouldn't have described herself as superstitious—she never even bothered to read her horoscope—but she couldn't help feeling that there was something inauspicious about showing up at the wrong address.

The more she thought about it, the more dejected she became. Not only that, but the rain was getting worse, and she didn't have an umbrella.

It's not as if there's anywhere to buy one around here, Elizabeth thought as she looked at the rows and rows of beautiful houses. *Oh, who cares? I probably couldn't afford one anyway.*

The only thing that kept Elizabeth from sinking too deep was the intense beauty of the city. She'd simply never seen architecture to compare. Everywhere she looked, her eye was caught by something extraordinary. It seemed like there were statues and public monuments on every corner.

She stopped to look at one of a horse and rider, but she couldn't make out the inscription; it was coated with hundreds of years' worth of soot. Elizabeth couldn't help being amazed at how, well, how *old* things seemed. Back in Sweet Valley, most of the buildings were new; an old building was one from the sixties. But here—Elizabeth could see that some of the buildings were *centuries* old. She stopped to read a blue metal plaque on the side of a house. Apparently a minor Victorian composer had written his finest works there.

Elizabeth hurried along, keeping her eyes peeled for more fascinating historical tidbits, but she was totally unprepared for the next plaque that she saw.

10 Downing Street? That's the prime minister's address! She stopped and stared at the huge iron gates that guarded the entrance. She'd once written an article about his stance on the Balkan position, but she'd never expected to be standing outside his house. She wanted to stay and see if the prime minister would come out, but she was afraid that the security guard would think there was something suspicious about her and shoo her away. Besides, she wanted to get to school.

She turned away from the gates and moved off down the street, which wasn't very crowded. It was now eleven in the morning, not a time for commuters or a lunch crowd to be milling about. There were a few people wandering, and Elizabeth was surprised at the different fashions they wore. There were some conservatively dressed, some in wild, supertrendy clothes, and some in plain jeans and jean jackets, just like back home.

Elizabeth pulled her cardigan more tightly around her, wishing she had her light down vest, which would be so snuggly warm right now. She'd even settle for her heaviest sweater. Anything to keep the chill off her skin. When she'd imagined walking down a street in London, she'd pictured herself in a smart trench coat and leather pumps, carrying an umbrella with a wooden handle—not exactly the image she was living up to now.

The temperature was chilly, the air damp, and Elizabeth swore that it was seeping inside her bones. No wonder the English drank so much tea; they needed it to warm them up! And suddenly the idea of hot and crunchy fish-and-chips sounded warm and comforting. Elizabeth was cold, wet, and hungry—three things she hated being.

The top of a building caught her eye, and Elizabeth felt excitement run up her spine. There it was! The building on the Web site, the building in the brochures that she'd been sent. It loomed out of the mist majestically, like a gorgeous gray stone castle. Elizabeth could see that even though it was in the heart of the city, manicured flower beds surrounded the buildings. The towers and outbuildings looked like something out of a medieval fairy tale, and for a second Elizabeth simply stood still and looked at it.

What am I waiting for? she wondered as she spotted a man at the door. *He's probably a security guard*, Elizabeth thought, and with a cry of relief she ran toward him.

"Is this the University of London?" she asked breathlessly as she dropped her duffel bag onto the concrete steps.

"Yes," he said, eyeing her with disapproval.

"Finally!" Elizabeth exclaimed. She almost collapsed in relief at his feet. "I'm here to register."

"Well, I'm afraid you can't do that till noon," the man said.

"I can't?" Elizabeth wailed.

"The administration buildings don't open until noon before the fall term begins. You've got a good hour, miss."

Elizabeth's stomach dropped. She thought about asking the man if he just so happened to have an extra umbrella, but she had a feeling he didn't. Or if he did, it would be broken. She was having that kind of morning.

Well, what the heck am I supposed to do for an hour? she wondered. All she wanted was to sign in, be shown her room, and collapse on a comfy bed with heavy quilts and soft, down pillows.

"I guess—I guess maybe I'll find a bench or—or take a walk or something," she mumbled to the man.

He shrugged. "Up to you, miss. One hour. If you'd like, you can leave your bags in the porters' lodge."

"That would be wonderful," Elizabeth said

gratefully. She followed him there, deposited the bags, and headed back into the rain.

Elizabeth clutched the piece of paper that Daphne had given her as if it possessed magical powers. She supposed it was a little soon to be popping up on Daphne's doorstep, but seeing as how she had nowhere else to go—and that she was too zonked to check out a museum or walk around—heading over to the hostel seemed the best bet.

"I wonder if I could take a shower there?" Elizabeth murmured to herself, imagining the hot water running down her back instead of the cold drizzle that was now splashing her in the face. Maybe Daphne would treat her to breakfast—after all, Elizabeth had let her sit at her table at the diner, hadn't she? That seemed like so long ago. She didn't like to ask for a handout, but the truth was that she was starving, and from Elizabeth's experience with bureaucracies, it would probably take all afternoon until her stipend came through. She wouldn't even consider parting with any of her own money—her pounds—even for a cup of steaming hot tea and a muffin at the small, cozy café she had just passed by.

Mr. Grove—the maintenance man at the school who had helped her store her luggage—

had also given her directions to the youth hostel, and this time Elizabeth had *triple* checked the address. Lucky for her it was within walking distance of the university.

As she headed down the street, Elizabeth was surprised to see just how crowded and busy London really was. Her school was nestled in a residential area, but now that she was in a shopping district, she was finally seeing the London she'd expected. It was nothing like Sweet Valley. Of course, Elizabeth knew that Sweet Valley was just a small town by comparison, but still, the difference was shocking. She'd never been in such a hustling-and-bustling kind of place before, and she wondered if she'd ever get used to the pace.

Elizabeth found that she was crossing her fingers that Daphne would be at the hostel and not out doing some sight-seeing. She was much lonelier than she would have thought possible. She knew that once she was involved with the mechanics of registering, she wouldn't have time to dwell on her problems, but right now, wandering around in the drizzle, she didn't seem to be able to think about anything else.

Get a grip and look at this gorgeous city, Elizabeth chastised herself. She tried to really take in the sights that she was passing. There were so many things that were exciting and new, she didn't want for choice. She wondered where the Tate was and the National Gallery. Elizabeth remembered an art-history professor telling her that it housed one of the greatest art collections in the world. Large black taxicabs whizzed by as she splashed across the street. Was she now in Piccadilly Circus? Elizabeth had seen countless images of its flashing neon signs, but she never expected to be walking in front of them. She wished she had a camera to take a photograph—perhaps she could pick up one of those disposable ones.

Unfortunately, there were too many people rushing about for her to really stop and check things out. And not only that, but the rain had gotten worse. She didn't know how much farther she could go without stopping for a rest or a cup of coffee. Her long hair was plastered uncomfortably to her face, and her socks and shoes were soaked, making a horrible sucking noise with each step she took.

At last Elizabeth saw the sign for the youth hostel on the other side of the street. She crossed hurriedly, nearly getting knocked over by a bright red double-decker bus. "Look the right way when you cross the street!" a man hollered over to her. She nodded, not sure if that was a friendly warning or an admonishment at a dumb American. She made a mental note to look *both* ways and walked inside the hostel.

The youth hostel was a pleasant surprise, shabby, but clean and comfortable. Elizabeth looked around the lobby with its overstuffed chairs and bright travel posters with a sigh of relief. She couldn't wait to collapse on Daphne's bed, hit the shower, and score some food.

"May I help you?" A girl of about her own age walked into the lobby from a back room, carrying a dust cloth in her hand.

"I hope so." Elizabeth smiled. "I'm looking for an American friend of mine, Daphne? Brown hair, tie-dyed T-shirt? She would have checked in about a half hour ago?"

"Oh, yes!" The girl nodded. "She *was* here, but we had to send her away since we have no space left. You see," she chattered brightly, unaware of the effect her words were having on Elizabeth, "we get filled up so quickly since we're so centrally located. People book weeks in advance."

"Oh," Elizabeth said slowly, her heart sinking.

"We directed her to a hostel out in Hampstead," the girl continued. "Since they're about thirty minutes out of London, they're not quite as busy as we are. You could go see if she's checked in there."

Elizabeth gnawed her lower lip. Thirty minutes there and back and she'd have used up her hour. Exhausting herself further in the process too. "Is it quicker by tube?" Elizabeth asked. "Perhaps it would be only a ten-minute ride."

"I meant by tube," the girl explained. "Actually, it might take forty minutes, what with the transfer I think you have to make."

The girl began plumping up the sofa pillows. "Are you visiting from America? I can never tell the Americans from the Canadians."

Elizabeth smiled. "Yes. California." She wiped a drop of water from her cheek. "So, um," she said, "does the rain ever let up?"

"Rain?" the girl repeated, peering out the window. "Are you calling *this* rain?" The girl looked out the window again and laughed. "You don't know London, then. This is *good* weather."

"It is?" Elizabeth glanced out the window. It was true that the rain had petered out to a drizzle, but it was hardly what she would call *good* weather. She felt a sudden sharp longing for the sunny skies of southern California. "I've got a half hour to kill . . . is there anything to see between here and the University of London?" She was hoping that perhaps she could sit and wait in the hostel, but the girl hadn't offered, and Elizabeth didn't want to be rude.

The girl smiled. "Why don't you pop round to Buckingham Palace and see if you can catch a glimpse of the queen?" She headed behind the registration desk and got out a map. "Just follow the Haymarket until you get to the Mall. You can't miss it."

The queen? Was she kidding or serious? Elizabeth honestly couldn't tell.

Elizabeth pressed her face against the wrought-iron fence that guarded the residence of the queen of England and stared at the guards, who were decked out in their full regimental regalia. The rain had fizzled out to just an occasional drop; still, Elizabeth was chilled to the bone.

She was overcome by the sense of history and pageantry that the entire scene represented. Although she'd never been to the White House, she'd seen pictures, and there was simply no way that a group of Secret Service men clad in dull government-issue gray suits could pass muster when compared with the queen's guards, resplendent in their red uniforms.

"I'll have to come back here when it's sunny out," Elizabeth told herself as she glanced down at the map the girl at the youth hostel had given her and studied some of the other suggestions that she'd jotted down. There were so many things to see. Perhaps she'd meet some other Americans once she was settled into university life, students who'd be interested in sight-seeing along with her.

She checked her watch. It was almost time! She took one last look at the palace and began the walk back to the university. The rain had let up, and there was even a little sunshine. Elizabeth tilted her face to catch the few rays that peeked through the clouds.

As she rounded a corner, she noticed a girl a few years younger than she was, dressed in rags and sitting with her back up against a post.

Poor thing, Elizabeth thought, feeling a tug at her heart. *She looks even worse than I do.* It was obvious that this girl hadn't had a meal in days and that she hadn't bathed in even longer. *Is she sleeping in the street?* Elizabeth wondered sadly. She certainly looked like she had been.

"Please, miss, spare some change?" the girl asked Elizabeth as she passed by.

Elizabeth bit her lip. She wasn't exactly in a position to be doling out money, but the girl looked so pitiful, and Elizabeth didn't have the heart to walk by without doing something.

Before she could change her mind, Elizabeth reached into her pocket and gave the girl one of the small, heavy gold coins that was a pound. She felt a tremor of fear as she passed the money over. Now she had barely anything.

What am I worried about? Elizabeth thought as she picked up her pace. *In a half hour I'll be settled at school, and then, after a shower and a nap, I'll go and have a nice hot meal in some fab pub with my new dorm mates. Besides, that poor girl needed that money even more than I did.*

And then at last she could explore the London of her dreams.

Chapter
Thirteen

As Elizabeth waited patiently in line in the University of London's registration room, she realized that everyone around her was registering for the summer session, which apparently was set to begin next week. No one was talking about the fall semester. A small shiver of worry tickled her brain. What if they didn't have a dorm room available? What if she had to come back in September? It was only June now, and the summer loomed in front of her, unknown and without focus.

Don't worry, she told herself, nudging her duffel bag a few inches ahead of her on the floor. She'd picked it up when she'd returned to the university. *You're here, you've got some problems with money, and surely they'll straighten things out. Surely there's a room somewhere in all of London for you, even if not in the castlelike dorm Nigel mentioned.*

You're an accepted student; they have to take you.

She'd finally arrived back at the university—*an hour* after they'd opened. Twice she'd turned in the wrong direction and had gotten totally lost. And once she'd been given wrong directions; whether on purpose or not, she didn't know. Now she was standing in a long ribbon of chattering English students, a line that snaked around and around until it reached the registration windows at the front of the room.

"Pardon?"

Elizabeth glanced up to find two cute guys in front of her, smiling at her.

"We need you to break a tie," said one of them, a tall, thin guy with shaggy blond hair. He was wearing an oversize concert T-shirt from a band Elizabeth didn't know and a pair of skintight corduroys, which Elizabeth thought looked very British—and cute. "I say that Shakespeare is the greatest writer ever, and my friend here says that Milton was. What's your opinion?"

This was exactly the kind of conversation Elizabeth had dreamed of having at SVU, but the majority of the student body had seemed to be more interested in debating where the best beach was or what café served the finest iced coffee.

"Shakespeare, definitely," Elizabeth replied, looking at her two new acquaintances. "Okay, I give you Milton's *Paradise Lost*, but Shakespeare still wins."

"Enough about literature," the blond guy said, with a smile that told Elizabeth the whole debate had merely been a ruse to get to talk to her. "Are you American?"

Elizabeth nodded.

He winked at his friend. "Well, I'm sure our fair American cousin wants to talk about more interesting things, like what club I'm going to take her dancing at tonight."

Elizabeth smiled for what felt like the first time since she'd discovered Jessica and Sam locked in each other's arms. Maybe he was serious, maybe not. . . . It didn't really matter. A conversation with a cute stranger was exactly what she needed.

"Oh, we're up," said the blond guy, tilting his head toward an empty registration window. "I do hope I'll run into you again."

"Bye." Elizabeth watched him and his friend jog up to the window, wondering if she would see him on campus. If he was any indication, it appeared that the students would be friendly to her. Once she opened her mouth, people would know that she wasn't English, and she hoped that didn't turn anyone away. It would be nice to make some new friends, people she'd never have had the chance to meet if she hadn't decided to attend the University of London.

Soon I'll probably be walking around here with a bunch of new friends. I'll know all the places to hang out, which professors are nice and which are difficult, the best place to grab a scone and some tea, the pubs people frequent. . . . She thought back to her friends at SVU. How they would envy her!

The school was even more beautiful on the inside than the outside had prepared her for. The building was easily centuries old, and Elizabeth had been thrilled to see the photos of famous British writers that lined the walls.

More exciting than that, however, had been the course packet she'd picked up at the start of the line. Milton, Shakespeare, Dickens, Austen. The names danced in front of her eyes like so many stars. Here she was in Dickens's very own city! She vowed to reread his novels and then walk through the very streets he'd described. *David Copperfield* would be first on her list. Or maybe *Oliver Twist?*

I can't believe that I'm really here, Elizabeth thought, flipping through the course packet. She was in Jane Austen's England. Shakespeare's England. The England of her own dreams. She'd spend the fall reading and writing and discussing literature with new friends and brilliant professors. She imagined herself with a thick Victorian novel by the Thames River, being inspired to write. . . .

"Next student, please," called a registration clerk, and Elizabeth flew to the window.

"Hi," Elizabeth said to the woman. She handed over her acceptance letter. "I'm here to register for the—"

"I'm afraid that you can't register here," the woman said, passing back the letter to Elizabeth.

"Why not?" Elizabeth asked, her fingers tightening on the envelope.

"You have to go to the registration desk for exchange students," the woman explained.

"Oh," Elizabeth said, relieved. For a moment she'd been terrified that there had been some terrible mistake.

"There really should be a sign posted," the woman conceded. "Go down the corridor, turn left, and down the stairs. Present this letter to Nikola Hudson. She's the one you want to talk to. Sorry about the mix-up."

It didn't take long for Elizabeth to find the registration desk for exchange students. Only one other student was there, and he was putting his papers away in his messenger bag, having already been processed.

"Nikola Hudson?" Elizabeth asked, smiling politely at the woman behind the desk. She was so tired that she could barely see straight, and she pushed her acceptance letter across the desk with a sigh. "The woman upstairs told me to see you," she explained. "I'm an exchange student."

"You've come to the right place, then." Nikola took the letter and scanned it carefully. "Hmmm. Except that you're here two months early."

Elizabeth felt her stomach tighten. "I, um, was just so eager—"

"You're lucky we have the space," the woman said. "Although you might have to double up with another student until your semester begins in late August."

Elizabeth nodded and let out a very deep breath. Everything was going to be okay. She watched Nikola type on the keyboard and frown at the computer. She typed more, clicked, and frowned more.

"Spell your last name, please," Nikola said, staring at the screen.

Elizabeth did.

She shook her head. "It's not coming up."

"Elizabeth Wakefield. I'm the exchange student from Sweet Valley University, Sweet Valley, California."

"If you're not popping up on this screen," Nikola said, "it means you need to see the bursar about getting your scholarship papers stamped. I can't register you until the bursar stamps your form and makes a notation on your record. Then you'll pop up on my registration list."

This was getting tired. She counted to five and told herself not to lose it.

"Up the stairs, to your right, down the hall," Nikola told her, pointing with her pen. "Once they take care of your scholarship, we'll be all set."

Elizabeth nodded and trudged wearily toward the steps.

All she could think about was that she'd have to climb up two flights of steps to get back to square one.

"Hmmm, that's strange," said Mrs. Stuart, the bursar, frowning as she flipped through a stack of computer printouts. "I don't see your name here."

"Really?" Elizabeth said faintly, her nerves frazzled.

She was getting more and more worn out by the second. At least Mrs. Stuart had turned out to be a nice warm, motherly type. After Elizabeth had finished pouring out her story, she'd sat her down and offered her a cup of Ceylon tea. According to Mrs. Stuart, the English believed there were very few things that couldn't be sorted out by drinking "a cuppa."

"Your name isn't in the records," Mrs. Stuart explained, shaking her head. "The system's always making mistakes. Now you pop right downstairs again and tell them that I said to process you. You need to get your housing situation sorted out. You look like you could do with a good rest. I'm sure I'll be able to sort this out; I'm just not sure that we can get to it today." She looked at her watch. "We're almost closing—"

"Almost closing?" Elizabeth didn't mean to interrupt, but she was shocked. How could it be almost time for them to close? *I guess she's right,* Elizabeth realized as she looked at the clock on the opposite wall. *No wonder I'm so exhausted.*

"Not to worry," Mrs. Stuart continued. "We don't want to keep you waiting that long." She scribbled a note on a piece of paper and handed it to Elizabeth. "What you want is a good night's rest. I've written a note telling the administrators to give you your housing assignment. Let's hope that by the time you wake up, everything will have been taken care of at this end."

"Thank you," Elizabeth said, trying to stifle a yawn. "You're right; I can't wait to get to sleep."

"You can't miss it," Mrs. Stuart said cheerily. "Just go downstairs, turn—"

"Right, follow the hall," Elizabeth finished under her breath as she left the room and began to walk down the stairs.

"Look, there has to be some mistake," Elizabeth insisted for the third time. "Mrs. Stuart said that you could sort this out later and that I could have my housing assignment now." Elizabeth knew that she was starting to whine, and she hated to start off on the wrong foot, but she just couldn't take any more.

"I'm sorry," Mr. Moore said once again. "But no matter how much I may want to help you, I can't give you your room assignment if I don't see you in the system."

Elizabeth was so tired that her legs were practically buckling underneath her. All she could think of was crawling into a warm bed. "Please," she begged. "I just want to go to—"

"I've found you," Mr. Moore interrupted.

Elizabeth sagged against the desk in relief. She could already feel the warmth of crisp cotton sheets sliding over her body. Her eyes closed as she imagined her room. *First a shower* . . .

"Ah, this is the problem," Mr. Moore continued.

"Problem? Problem?" Elizabeth's eyes flew wide open.

"Apparently your place has been given to a student from UCLA." Mr. Moore looked genuinely surprised as he looked from the computer screen to Elizabeth. "It seems that you didn't respond to the acceptance letter by the deadline, so you forfeited your place and scholarship."

Elizabeth's entire body stilled.

"But I—," she whispered weakly.

It was true. She hadn't responded. Normally she was the type of person who paid her bills the day she received them, who did her homework assignments the moment they were passed out, who did her holiday shopping in September. Yet she'd been so busy thinking about her and Sam's fledgling relationship, so busy trying to ignore that she'd applied in the first place, she'd overlooked the respond-by date.

Elizabeth felt like the floor was swallowing her up. She stared at Mr. Moore in total shock. "There must be some mistake," she protested feebly, knowing in her heart that wasn't true. Clammy sweat broke out on her back as she tried to come up with something that would justify her lack of action.

"I wish there was something I could do, but I'm afraid my hands are tied." Mr. Moore shook his head.

"Please," Elizabeth pleaded. She was dangerously close to tears. "Can't this be fixed somehow? I mean, I *was* accepted." She thrust the letter at him. If they'd given away her place, surely they could make room for her now that she was here.

"I understand." Mr. Moore shook his head again. "This must be a terrible shock, but there's really nothing I can do."

"I . . . I . . ." Elizabeth was at a total loss. She'd never felt so helpless in her entire life. "There must be *something*. . . ."

"Even if I could bend the rules, we're over-extended as it is for the fall semester," he explained helplessly. "I've just assigned the last dormitory room we had."

"But Nikola, one of the clerks, mentioned you had lots of space for the summer and . . ."

"She was mistaken, I'm afraid," he said. "Perhaps she hasn't looked at the updated housing database. We have a waiting list of at least sixty students already. We had a twenty-five percent increase in students staying on for the summer session."

"Oh," Elizabeth said, her throat tightening.

"I'm very sorry, but we have to close now. I'm afraid there's nothing I can do for you." He sighed. "Do you have friends or family here in London, perhaps?"

"No—No, I don't," she said, dazed.

He raised his hands and shrugged. "If we had only known you were intending on coming . . ." He trailed off, then stood and began shuffling papers. Elizabeth had no choice but to walk out.

Students were filing out of the building, and she allowed herself to be pushed along with them. She was so disoriented that she didn't even notice where she was until she was outside on the pavement.

She turned back to the door. She *had* to fight this. There was no way that she could leave things as they were. Where would she go from here? Elizabeth felt dizzy just thinking about it.

"Sorry," a young guy said when she turned and tried to go back inside. "We're closing for the night." He shut the door with a polite smile, and Elizabeth was left by herself on the stone steps as a soft rain started to fall.

Elizabeth felt faint. *Okay, keep it together,* she told herself. There had to be some way out of this nightmare.

Maybe she could call her friend Nina and she could wire her some money, Elizabeth thought as she reached frantically for her cell phone. She punched in the numbers, but the call didn't go through.

Of course, you fool. Your cell phone isn't going to work in England.

Elizabeth stumbled down the steps and onto the street. She'd lost her place at the university, she didn't have any money, and she couldn't even use her phone.

Fear swirled around her, and she resisted the urge to collapse on the street. She knew she had to figure out something, but she was so scared that she was having a hard time thinking. She walked down the street, barely noticing where she was going. The rain was coming down harder, and she shivered, pressing her duffel against her chest and trying to shield herself from the weather.

All right. Elizabeth tried to rein in her thoughts. *I've got to find some way out of this. What did Mrs. Stuart say? That a cup of tea could cure anything? Well, it's worth a try.*

Elizabeth looked around for a place where she could get something to drink. She really didn't put much faith in Mrs. Stuart's cure-all, but she had no other options.

And money aside, she needed to get out of the rain.

What was she going to do?

Chapter Fourteen

"I'd like a cup of tea, please, with two sugars and extra lemon," Elizabeth announced to the young woman behind the counter. It hadn't taken her too long before she'd found a small self-service café, and after carefully checking the prices that were chalked on the menu, she'd decided that she could afford to stay.

"Extra lemon?" The girl behind the counter frowned at Elizabeth as she poured a cup of tea. She looked at Elizabeth like she'd asked for extra cyanide.

"That's right," Elizabeth replied, confused. She watched as the girl poured a generous measure of cream into her tea. *Guess they don't use lemon here,* she thought with a shrug as she carried the tea over to a small table and sat down.

Okay, the important thing is to remain calm,

Elizabeth told herself as she sipped. *I just have to keep reminding myself that I've dealt with some pretty serious situations before,* she thought, fighting down a tremor of fear as she took her journal out of her knapsack and opened it to a fresh page. She began making a list of things she had to do. Was there any way that she could salvage the situation? Could she stay in England without being in school? *Yeah, right.* Elizabeth grimaced. *By the end of the week I'll be like that poor beggar this morning.*

Elizabeth shook her head in dismay. Clearly she'd have to figure out something. Maybe she could work out a deal with the school? What she needed to do, she decided, was to get on-line and e-mail Professor Sedder at SVU. Why hadn't she thought of that before? It was just possible that he'd be able to help her get the whole nightmare sorted out and that she'd be reinstated in the program, with a place to live *and* the stipend she'd been promised.

She glanced at her watch and calculated the time change. He was probably just waking up right around now. Swallowing the last of her tea, she put her journal back in her bag. She wasn't looking forward to hitting the streets again—the weather was miserable, and she grimaced at the thought of walking in the rain again. She'd seen enough rain in the past eight hours to last her a lifetime.

With a deep sigh Elizabeth left the café and started walking briskly down the crowded street. She was pretty sure that she'd passed some signs for Charing Cross Road before. Hadn't Daphne told her that was a pretty lively area? She could probably find a cybercafé there. Unfortunately she wasn't seeing any signs now, and the rain was starting to fall a little harder.

This is so totally beat, Elizabeth thought as she crossed the street. Why hadn't she asked the girl at the café if there were any cybercafés nearby?

Clunk!

"Pardon," said the guy who Elizabeth had banged into.

"Excuse me," Elizabeth said. The guy was around her age, with bright pink hair, and he was dressed in leather. Hadn't the punk look ended about twenty years ago? *Guess not,* Elizabeth thought. "Do you know where I could find a cybercafé around here?" she asked as she straightened herself up. "I'm kind of lost, and I need to find someplace to log on."

"You what?" the guy asked, looking at her like she was crazy. Elizabeth was getting tired of people reacting to her that way.

"I asked if you knew someplace where I could get on-line," Elizabeth said through gritted teeth.

"On where?" he squawked.

"Never mind," Elizabeth muttered as she pushed passed him. Well, what did she expect from a guy who dyed his hair pink? She'd have to ask someone else.

"Excuse me." Elizabeth flashed her best smile at a young stockbroker type who was unlocking the door to his Jaguar.

"Yes?" He quirked an eyebrow as he tossed an expensive leather briefcase onto the backseat.

"I was wondering if you could tell me how to get to Charing Cross," Elizabeth said.

"That's miles from here." He looked at her in surprise. "You're best off taking a cab. There should be a taxi rank around here somewhere." He gestured vaguely with his hand before jumping in his car and roaring off.

Elizabeth's shoulders slumped as she stared at the departing Jaguar. Of course she wouldn't have *accepted* a ride with him, but he could at least have *asked* if she could use one. Where was that famous English courtesy she'd always heard so much about?

She had a feeling that she should bag the Charing Cross idea. Clearly she'd gotten her bearings wrong, and besides, that couldn't be the only place that had what she needed. *Maybe I should just forget the whole thing,* Elizabeth thought, looking up at the sky. The rain was getting worse, and

170

not only that, it was starting to get late. *But when will I get in touch with Professor Sedder?* She wanted to take care of things as soon as possible, and she was sure that he'd be able to help her get to the bottom of the mess that she was in.

Wait a minute! Elizabeth stopped suddenly in the middle of the pavement. What was she thinking of? She *couldn't* get in touch with Professor Sedder. To get in touch with him was ultimately to get in touch with her parents. They'd probably be all over him like white on rice, and if he knew where she was, well, Elizabeth was sure he would tell them.

Idiot, she chastised herself. *You already told them you were headed to the University of London. They* already *know.*

What was she expecting the professor to do anyway? Call the university, which he had no connection to, and tell them they had to let her in, even though she blew the deadline to respond? He'd tell her to grow up and that he had better things to do than harm his reputation further by associating with her.

I guess I don't have to worry about finding a cybercafé after all, Elizabeth thought dejectedly. Strangely enough, she wasn't too upset about the fact that she couldn't contact Sedder. In her heart of hearts, Elizabeth didn't want her parents to know where she was. She could just imagine them flying out on the next plane, determined to drag her home by her ears so that she could properly apologize to Jessica. After all, they'd flown from California to Illinois because of Jessica's stupid busted ankle. What would keep them from flying to London to drag their wayward daughter home?

She'd lost her place in the program, but she'd also won her total freedom from her family.

No one knew where she was now.

No one.

Elizabeth shivered. That wasn't as intriguing as it sounded a second ago. She had no money, no credit cards, no suitable clothing, and nowhere to stay for the night.

She plodded on through the busy London streets, toward where, she had no clue. Not even her crumpled-up map could help her—she could barely make out the tiny lettering in the growing darkness, and she had no idea where she was. *I need one of those you-are-here arrows.*

She remembered the youth hostel that she'd visited earlier that afternoon. At the time it had seemed a trifle drab, but now she looked back on it as if it had been the finest four-star hotel. *If only they had room,* Elizabeth thought longingly.

She was starting to become frightened. Whatever other problems she might have, none was more pressing than the need to find somewhere to sleep for the night. The idea of spending the night outside on the London streets was too terrifying to even consider, and Elizabeth firmly pushed an image of herself curled up on a bench out of her mind. Even the fact that she'd lost her scholarship paled in comparison.

Maybe she *should* go back to the youth hostel. Okay, so they didn't have any rooms, but they might be able to suggest a hotel, although Elizabeth couldn't imagine what kind of place would fit in with her budget. Well, she'd head over that way; if she had her bearings right *this* time, it was only about ten blocks from where she was standing. At least she had a direction to move in, and she'd keep her eye out for a cheap hotel along the way.

As she walked, she found herself getting used to people pushing past her, jostling her arms, and stepping on the heels of her shoes. She thought of what it was like to walk down Main Street in Sweet Valley. Even though the city wasn't even a tenth the size of London, the pavements seemed twice as wide, or maybe it was just that nobody pushed her off them as they jockeyed for position.

Why were they all rushing around anyway? This wasn't the London of her dreams. Then she let out a small laugh. She'd wanted to spend time reading the novels of Dickens—not living the downtrodden life of one of his characters.

The rain started coming down harder, and she paused inside a doorway to shield herself from the grape-size drops. *I can't go on like this,* she almost whimpered. Things hadn't been going well since she'd landed in England, but now they were decidedly grim. It was one thing to show up at the *wrong* address like she had earlier in the day, quite another to not even *have* an address to go to.

Elizabeth huddled in the doorway as she watched the crowds negotiate the pavement, fighting for space with their huge umbrellas. If she didn't feel so lost and forlorn, she would have found the spectacle fascinating. She couldn't remember the last time she'd been in such a big city before, and she'd certainly never been anyplace even remotely like London in her life.

The rain started to come down in heavy sheets, and Elizabeth stepped back farther into a corner. She saw a sign flashing on the other side of the street and squinted to make out what it said.

"Rooms for rent, cheapest daily rates in London," Elizabeth read out loud. Cheapest daily rates? That sounded good. How much could the place cost? The youth hostel had been only a few pounds a night. She was sure that these rooms cost more, but could it be that much more? From the outside, the motel or whatever it was didn't look very fancy. It was a far cry from some of the exclusive hotels that she'd passed earlier in the day. In fact, it looked like some of the small motels that she'd stayed in recently on her road trip.

Elizabeth decided to make a run for it. She held her duffel over her head as she ran across the street. She pushed open the door of the hotel; a tinkle of bells announced her. Elizabeth looked around at the brightly lit lobby. The walls were painted a pale blue, and there were plenty of over-stuffed couches upholstered in a cheery cabbage-rose print. It was true that the walls were peeling a little and the couches were stained, but Elizabeth didn't care. Just the thought of taking a warm shower and collapsing on a bed was enough to make her swoon.

"May I help you?" the woman behind the reception desk asked. She peered over the rim of her glasses at Elizabeth. She seemed friendly enough, but it was clear that she was shocked at Elizabeth's appearance.

I must look like something the cat dragged in, Elizabeth thought, flushing in embarrassment as she attempted to smooth down her hair, which was tangled beyond repair. She knew that she was dripping all over the floor, but there was nothing she could do about it.

"Might I be of assistance?" the woman asked dubiously.

"I hope so." Elizabeth took a couple of steps forward. "The sign outside says that you have the cheapest rooms in London. Is that true?" Her teeth had begun to chatter so loudly that she wondered if the woman could even understand what she was saying. "Do you have any rooms available?"

"Oh, yes, indeed, we have several," the woman answered. From the expression on her face Elizabeth guessed that she wished she could say that they were all booked.

"How much are they?" Elizabeth asked as she dumped her backpack and duffel on the floor. She was already imagining how good it would feel to crawl under the covers. Maybe the woman would take pity on her and send up a cup of tea.

"Fifty pounds a night, including full English breakfast," the woman said as she passed the register across the desk. "Would you be staying for one night or two?"

"Try none," Elizabeth muttered, staring at the woman openmouthed. *Fifty pounds?* She did a quick calculation. That was like a hundred dollars! Elizabeth thought of the last motel that she'd stayed in before fleeing the States. It hadn't been anywhere near that expensive. Of course, she'd been on the outskirts of Springfield too, not exactly one of the major cities in the world, but still . . .

"I'm sure you'll find that our prices are very competitive," the woman said.

"I'm sure," Elizabeth murmured as she backed toward the door. Maybe the prices were competitive, but they were still way beyond her. "I just don't have much money on me."

Where to now? Elizabeth looked up and down the windblown street. She didn't have the energy to walk to the youth hostel. Besides, it was probably a useless excursion anyway. She was afraid to spend any more money getting something to eat or drink, but she couldn't just pound the pavement forever.

Elizabeth glanced down the street and was relieved to see an entrance to the tube. She could hang out there for a few minutes while she figured out what else to do; at least it was warm and dry.

She hurried down the steps and into the well-lit station. Should she buy a ticket and ride for a while? Elizabeth started to study the map, but her eye was caught by a boldly colored poster on the opposite wall, advertising an employment office. She walked over to read it more closely.

Wilson's Employment, offering a wide range of opportunities for the motivated individual. Elizabeth glanced at the address printed in bright red on the bottom of the poster. Apparently it was just outside the tube station and—she glanced at her watch—open for another twenty minutes. If she dashed up the stairs, she'd be able to make it in no time.

Well, I'm certainly one highly motivated individual, Elizabeth thought as she headed toward the exit. *In fact, they don't come any more motivated than this!*

She raced up the steps, feeling more hopeful than she had in hours.

A job was all she needed. She'd get an advance on her paycheck, find a cheap place to stay, and figure out the rest. Somehow, some way, she'd figure out the rest.

She had to.

"In what field are you looking for work, precisely?" Ms. Dunne smiled frostily at Elizabeth. She flicked a small piece of lint off her collar and straightened the papers on her desk, which were stacked with military precision.

How about any field that will take me? Elizabeth smiled back uncertainly as she shifted uncomfortably in the overstuffed chair that Ms. Dunne had insisted that she sit in.

She'd arrived at Wilson's just as they were locking up for the night. She'd practically had to beg on her hands and knees to get Ms. Dunne to interview her, but now that she'd finally convinced her, she wasn't sure that it was such a great idea after all.

For one thing, Wilson's was much more up-scale than Elizabeth was expecting—the office was decorated in an incredibly luxurious style with antiques and fancy-looking paintings decorating the walls. Ms. Dunne had taken one look at Elizabeth's dripping wet hair and tactfully led her away from the Louis the Fourteenth settee to the upholstered chair.

Something tells me that they won't be able to help me land a temp job, Elizabeth thought. She resisted the urge to wipe the sweat that was gathering on her forehead. The office was unpleasantly over-heated, and after running around in the cool, damp weather for the past few hours, the temperature was making Elizabeth feel slightly sick.

"Well?" Ms. Dunne managed to raise one perfectly arched eyebrow and look down her nose at the same time. "What line of work are you most interested in pursuing?" She pursed her lips and waited for Elizabeth to respond.

"Um, well, really I was looking for anything I could get," Elizabeth said as confidently as she could. She was having a hard time keeping herself from squirming under Ms. Dunne's eagle-eyed gaze. "You see, I kind of have an emergency situation here."

"Really?" Ms. Dunne raised her other eyebrow. "An emergency?" She looked extremely skeptical. "I see," she said slowly. "Might I see your curriculum vitae?"

"My curriculum vitae?" Elizabeth frowned. She had no idea what Ms. Dunne was talking about; she only knew that she was feeling more and more out of place by the second. "Oh! You mean my *résumé*," Elizabeth realized suddenly. "I don't exactly have one with me."

Elizabeth couldn't blame Ms. Dunne for looking at her like she was some kind of bum. Elizabeth had never shown up for a job interview like this before. She thought back to the last interview she'd gone on in Sweet Valley. She'd arrived a half hour early in a skirt and blouse. Not only did she have her résumé neatly printed out, but she'd also armed herself with glowing recommendations from her past three employers. Elizabeth could hardly believe that had been just a few months ago. It seemed like it was another lifetime.

"I see." Ms. Dunne's voice became distinctly more glacial. "Well, let's at least get some of your particulars, shall we?"

"Of course," Elizabeth murmured. She had no idea what her "particulars" were, but she didn't feel like asking and making an even bigger fool of herself than she already had.

"Perhaps it would be best if you just gave me your working papers, and we could go from there," Ms. Dunne said, extending a perfectly manicured hand.

"Working papers?" Elizabeth stared at her as if she were speaking Chinese. *Working papers?* Of course she needed working papers if she was going to get a job! She flashed back to the scene that morning at immigration. How could she have forgotten? Had her brain gone on permanent vacation?

"I'm sorry," Elizabeth said in a small voice. "But you see, I don't really have working papers." She wished that she could dissolve into the carpet. She'd never felt so incompetent in her life. What had happened to the practical, resourceful girl that she'd been a week ago? *That* girl wouldn't be in this situation. *That* girl would find some way out of this endless nightmare.

Wait a minute, she thought, remembering something Daphne had said. Something about finding work off the books. Hadn't she said that she was going to look for work as a maid or dishwasher if she was short of bucks? Well, Elizabeth would just have to do the same. There had to be plenty of places that were short of staff for one reason or another and would be happy to take someone on for a few days. She'd passed quite a few restaurants on the short walk from the tube to Wilson's.

Yes! She'd just start knocking on doors. . . . *Forget a regular restaurant,* she realized. *You should get a job in a* hotel *restaurant!*

If she got a job in a hotel, not only could she solve her cash-flow problem, but she could probably score a room for the night too. Elizabeth breathed a sigh of relief. She was starting to see a way out of this horrible situation. Maybe, just maybe things would work out after all.

"You don't have any working papers?" Ms. Dunne interrupted her thoughts. "In that case, I'm afraid that I really can't help you, dear." For an instant she looked almost sorry for Elizabeth.

"Oh, I think maybe you can." Elizabeth sat up. "Could you recommend a good hotel near here?"

Chapter Fifteen

Elizabeth paused uncertainly in front of the ornate carved door and glanced down at the piece of paper where Ms. Dunne had scribbled the name of the nearest hotel. This was the place, all right. Only it looked more like a private club than a hotel.

Where was the blinking sign that announced if they had vacancies? Where was the luggage cart? At the other hotels that she'd passed earlier in the day, there'd always been a bevy of doormen dressed in gold-braided uniforms guarding the entrance. If she craned her head, she could see a discreet brass sign that was engraved with the name of the hotel, but other than that there was nothing to indicate it was anything other than somebody's home—a very *rich* somebody's home.

The carved door opened suddenly, and a couple

dressed to the nines floated out on a cloud of expensive perfume. Elizabeth's eyes were temporarily blinded by the rows and rows of diamonds that encircled the woman's neck. She stared as the man paused for a second to open an elegant gold cigarette case; he lit a match, then tossed it in the street. She jumped back just in time to avoid being burned. She watched as the couple hopped into a waiting luxury car.

Don't they have any motels in this town? Elizabeth wondered. She'd pictured herself helping out in the kind of roadside place that she'd stayed in on her trip from Sweet Valley to Illinois, but she was finally beginning to understand that England was not America.

Should she even bother trying at this place? Would they laugh at her? She'd had enough humiliation in the past few hours to last her for the rest of her life. *Oh, who cares if they laugh,* Elizabeth thought. She didn't have the luxury of pride. Things were getting desperate. Well, actually, they'd gotten desperate *hours* ago. She simply had to find a solution for the night, and she knew that the old Elizabeth—the one who hadn't been beaten down by losing her boyfriend, leaving her home, and wandering in the rain—the *old* Elizabeth wouldn't stop trying until she landed something.

Hey, she thought as she squared her shoulders and walked up the few steps to the door. *For all I know, the lady in the luxury car needs help folding her clothes or something.*

Elizabeth tugged at the door handle, but it was surprisingly heavy, and she couldn't budge it. She braced her shoulder against the door and shoved hard; the door gave way, and she tumbled into the lobby.

She'd never seen anything like it before. Her feet sank into the Persian carpet, which was thicker and more plush than a down comforter. Huge bouquets perfumed the air, and soft light was provided by the enormous crystal chandeliers that hung from the ceiling. Elizabeth gasped as she looked up at them. They were as beautiful as the diamond necklace that the woman in the car had been wearing.

"May I help you?" a snooty type in a pinstripe cutaway asked as he looked her up and down.

It seemed to Elizabeth that she'd been asked that question more in the past few hours than she'd ever been asked it in her entire life before. The only problem was that the answer usually turned out to be that *no,* nobody could help her.

Elizabeth took a deep breath and stood as straight as she possibly could. She tried to act like there was nothing unusual in her appearance or what she was about to ask.

"I'd like to speak to the manager, please," she said, trying to ignore the puddle she was making on the carpet.

"I am the manager," the man replied.

Elizabeth could see that although he was baffled by her wet-dishrag appearance, nothing would stop him from behaving with perfect propriety. *He may think I'm crazy, but at least he won't laugh at me,* she tried to reassure herself.

"I was wondering if you had any positions available," Elizabeth said, unable to keep her voice from squeaking.

"Positions?" The manager raised his eyebrows. "Ah, I see. You are inquiring about whether we are taking on any staff at the moment?"

"Right." Elizabeth nodded vigorously. "I mean, yes, that's it exactly."

"Well, then, I must tell you that we have several positions available."

Elizabeth's spirits rose, and she nearly collapsed in relief. She stared at the manager as if he were her savior.

"For highly skilled individuals who've completed their training at any one of the accredited butler and servant training schools," he finished smoothly, completely dashing Elizabeth's hopes. "Although, of course," he continued, "we do favor those applicants who've recently graduated

186

from Madame Paulett's in Paris or Jeeves Academy in Dublin."

"I see," Elizabeth said slowly. She was becoming uncomfortably familiar with squirming in front of people, and it wasn't a feeling that she liked. Still, maybe the manager would take pity on her. Maybe he could recommend someplace else she might go, or maybe he would offer her a cup of tea.

"May I say," the manager went on, "that I consider it extremely bad taste for you to enter an establishment like this, dressed the way you are, and ask about employment."

Guess I won't be getting any tea! Elizabeth blushed hotly as she stared at the manager in dismay. She almost took umbrage at his remarks—she definitely knew how to look for a job the right way—but how could she fault him? He was right. *But what about some good, old-fashioned tea and sympathy?* She turned and pushed out the door and found herself back in the cold drizzle that seemed to be London's constant weather. She supposed she should feel embarrassed, but at this point she was past caring. If she didn't find a solution to her problems soon, she was going to be in very serious trouble.

Where to now? Elizabeth looked up and down the street. She didn't have a clue what she should do next. She didn't know where to go or what to do when she got there. She only knew that she had to do *something* and find *somewhere*.

Elizabeth wouldn't let herself get panicky. She knew that she had to stay positive if she was going to be able to make things work. But knowing that didn't stop a few tears from falling down her face as she shouldered her packs and started off down the road.

Elizabeth was so tired that she could barely stand. She kept bumping into people as she walked gracelessly down the street, staring at the pavement as though it held answers. She barely had the energy to put one foot in front of the other, and she desperately wanted to sit down, but she was afraid that if she settled herself on one of the benches she saw, she would fall asleep.

"Ow!" Elizabeth cried. Two men smoking cigars and speaking a foreign language rapidly dashed by her, nearly knocking her over. She managed to save herself by flinging out her hands, but she scraped them badly on the pavement. "Thanks a lot!" Elizabeth cried after them as they jumped into a waiting car and drove away. She stared at the license plate . . . something was different about it. It was an embassy plate.

Elizabeth stood stock-still in the middle of the

pavement. The embassy! Should she go to the American embassy? Wouldn't they have to take her in for the night? She remembered a friend who'd had his passport stolen while backpacking through Europe. He had gone to the American embassy and thrown himself on their mercy. Supposing she did the same? Would they find her a bed for the night? What if they called her parents?

She shook her head. She just couldn't risk doing something that would put her in contact with them. It hurt to think that way, but Elizabeth knew that things had changed the second she boarded the plane to England. She loved her parents, and she always would, but she needed to find out who she was outside of them, outside of Jessica, outside of SVU, and outside of Sweet Valley.

If things were going to work out for her in London, she was going to have to do it on her own. Making contact with the embassy was out.

I'm going to find some way out of this, Elizabeth vowed. *No matter what it takes, I'm going to find some way!*

If she could only get some rest. Everything else would fall into place if she could only find a place to sleep.

"Are you all right, dear?" A kindly faced older woman stopped and looked at her closely.

"I need a place to stay," Elizabeth blurted out.

"I only have a few pounds," she couldn't stop herself from adding. Elizabeth knew that she should be embarrassed that she was telling her problems to a stranger, but she was past caring about formalities.

"Have you thought about trying a youth hostel, dear?" the woman asked. She patted Elizabeth on the shoulder, and Elizabeth nearly burst into tears at the tenderness in her touch. People had been nasty to her for so long that she had forgotten how powerful simple human kindness could be.

"Yes," Elizabeth replied. "But the one I went to was full; my friend couldn't find a place there, and she—" Elizabeth nearly kicked herself. How could she have been so stupid? Didn't the youth hostel say that they'd directed Daphne to another one thirty minutes outside London? Elizabeth frantically searched in her backpack for the piece of paper that the woman at the youth hostel had given her. Granted, she might spend all her money just getting out to the town, but perhaps Daphne could loan her some money, an IOU, until Elizabeth could get herself settled.

"Do you know where this is?" Elizabeth asked, thrusting the paper in the other woman's face. "This is a youth hostel that I think my friend is at." She was feeling almost hysterical with relief.

Daphne could surely lend her a few bucks, if not help her find a job, and in any case, she'd be able to get something to eat and go to sleep. She could deal with the rest of her problems in the morning.

"Why, yes, I do know where that is," the woman said, studying the address. "That's quite a ways from here. It's on the outskirts of London in a town called Hampstead. You'll need to take the tube. The stop you want is called Hampstead too. There's a tube station just across the traffic lights, over there." She gestured with the slip of paper.

"Thank you!" Elizabeth had to hold herself back from hugging the woman. She turned on her heel and ran for the tube.

Elizabeth relaxed against the soft blue plush of the tube seats and breathed a sigh of relief. Once she arrived at the youth hostel, she'd ask to see Daphne and hopefully be able to get herself a room and take a nap and then a shower. She knew she was expecting a lot from a girl she barely knew, but Daphne had been awfully nice, and Elizabeth was sure she wouldn't turn her away. It would be late by then, but perhaps there would be a sand-wich shop nearby, and she could get something to tide her over until tomorrow, when she'd definitely need plenty of energy to start job hunting.

Okay, so today totally blew, Elizabeth thought as

the train roared through the darkness. *But at least I learned a couple of things—I learned that I can take care of myself no matter what happens, and I learned that next time I go anywhere, I'm packing a feather bed and an umbrella!*

She had to fight to stay awake. The past few hours—ever since she found out that she didn't have a place at the University of London—she'd been functioning on pure adrenaline. Now that the end was in sight, her considerable nervous energy had evaporated, and she couldn't remember ever feeling so tired and drained.

I wonder where I'll find a job, she thought hazily. She'd worked at Sedona, a cosmetics store, when she was in high school, and she had several years of lifeguard experience. But the kind of jobs she would be qualified for without a work permit were things like waitressing and dish washing, occupations she knew little about except for the fact that they were exhausting. And was working off the books something she really wanted to do anyway?

It's not like I have a choice. But things will be all right, she told herself, rubbing the damp out of her sweater's sleeves. *You're heading somewhere with a plan for right now, for tonight, and that's good enough.*

Elizabeth craned her head to study the brightly colored map on the opposite wall. Only two more stops now. It seemed like she'd been riding the tube forever, and she was impatient to arrive. She tried halfheartedly to keep herself occupied by reading *Pride and Prejudice*, but the text that normally was so rich in meaning for her held little interest right now. When she realized she had read the same paragraph three times, she gave up and put the dog-eared book away.

As the train pulled into the Hampstead station, Elizabeth got slowly to her feet. Her legs felt like she was moving through molasses as she dragged herself up the stairs and out into the cooling summer night.

Thankfully the youth hostel was only one or two blocks from the tube, so she didn't have far to go. Elizabeth glanced at the directions that the clerk at the other youth hostel had scribbled down and trudged off—hoping she was going in the right direction for once.

The rain had faded to a bearable drizzle, and the air was refreshing and pleasant. Elizabeth looked around as she walked, surprised at how beautiful the neighborhood was. Much quieter and calmer than the busy streets of central London that she'd left behind.

There was an enormous park to her left, and she looked through the wrought-iron gates longingly. Maybe after she was all settled in and she'd dealt with all her problems, she could come back and have a picnic under that weeping cherry willow. Elizabeth paused and pressed her face against the cold iron fence. She imagined what it would be like to have a date with one of the English guys that she'd seen at school earlier. They'd bring bread for the ducks, and after they'd finished their own lunch, they'd take a boat out on that pond while he recited Shakespeare sonnets to her. Elizabeth frowned. What the heck was she thinking?

Stop! Reality check! Elizabeth shook her head to clear away the vision. *One thing at a time here. I've got to get a bed for the night before I start worrying about dates that I'm not even ready for!*

Still, it was the first time in hours that she'd been able to think about anything other than her immediate problems, and she was feeling better by the second as she approached the welcoming lights of the youth hostel.

Even though she was half dead from exhaustion, Elizabeth practically skipped the last few steps to the hostel entrance. She bounded through the door on the last of her nervous energy and tapped on the bell at the unstaffed reception desk before collapsing on a tattered but extra-comfortable couch in the entryway. A couple speaking French were playing cards at a table a few feet away, and a group of German-speaking teenagers walked by and headed up the stairs.

"May I help you?" A girl around her own age parted a pair of beaded curtains that separated an employees-only area from the reception area and poked her head through.

"Yes," Elizabeth said with a smile. She stretched her legs out in front of her as the girl sat behind a small, makeshift reception desk. "One of my friends is here, and I wondered if you could call her room and tell her I'm in the lobby? Her name is Daphne," Elizabeth explained, only now realizing she didn't know Daphne's last name. "She checked in sometime today, probably early this afternoon. She's American, like me."

"I'm afraid we don't have telephones in our rooms here," the girl said. "Daphne, you said?" The girl furrowed her brow and began flipping through a stack of papers on the desk. Elizabeth nodded, her spirits lifting with every word. Everything was going to be okay.

"I'm sorry—we don't have anyone by that name registered today." She shrugged, an apologetic smile on her face. "It's just that we have so many people here now that it's summer, especially Americans. If you're sure she came here and she's not on this list, then she must have been turned away."

Elizabeth bolted upright. *Turned away . . .*

The words repeated themselves in Elizabeth's head over and over. She hadn't even considered that as a possibility.

"We've been completely booked all week," the girl went on. "Not even a water closet is available," she said, trying to make a joke.

It was then that Elizabeth realized she was in trouble. Serious, dangerous trouble. Any hope of sharing a room with Daphne—or at the least, bumming a few bucks from her—was gone. She had spent her last few pounds on the train fare here, to Hampstead. She had nothing left. She knew no one.

"The fire chief was here yesterday, as a matter of fact, and he gave us a warning about too many people," the girl went on, obviously noting Elizabeth's despair. "Were you needing a room?"

Elizabeth couldn't speak. She could only nod.

"Oh, I'm truly sorry," the girl said sincerely. "You see, most people call to book ahead . . . we're one of the more popular hostels. If you'd given us a ring a couple of days ago, we might have been able to help, but now?" She spread her hands in a gesture of futility. "I know for a fact that all the hostels within thirty miles are booked."

"I'm begging you," Elizabeth pleaded, her fingers digging into the couch fabric. "Just for tonight. I—"

"Oh, if there was any way I could help you, I would," the girl whispered under her breath. "But I share a room with two other girls, and our supervisor would murder us if we took in a guest—not to mention I'm on probation already for being caught napping on the job last week. I'm afraid you're on your own."

"Thank you," Elizabeth managed to say. "Thanks anyway." She got up off the couch, moving slowly as if she were in a dream. But she knew this wasn't a dream. This was a nightmare.

Elizabeth walked past the iron gates of the park that she'd passed only moments before on her way to the hostel. Only this time she wasn't daydreaming about romantic picnics. This time her brain was too numb to think about much of anything at all.

She stared blindly ahead as she put one foot in front of the other and stumbled forward along the pavement. Even though she knew it was useless, she took out her wallet and fingered the few coins that were there. Not only did she know exactly how much she had, down to the last pence, but she also knew that it would barely buy her a bowl of soup, let alone a room for the night.

She squinted in the darkness, trying to make out the faces on the one bill she had left. If only there was a streetlamp nearby . . .

There wasn't, but a shaft of moonlight glowed

down on her just as the rain began to fizzle to a stop.

It was then that Elizabeth noticed a massive, imposing old building—almost a small castle, really—set back on the far side of the park. The building looked like something out of a fairy tale, with exquisite architecture and turrets rising out of the inky black mist. It was much too big to be a private house. *Could it be a bed-and-breakfast?* Elizabeth wondered. Perhaps she could throw herself on the owner's mercy, explain her situation. Maybe the owner would feel so bad for her and let her spend the night in a maid's room?

"I'll wash the dishes," she said through gritted teeth, hoisting her bags once more and striding toward the immaculate grounds on feet that were blistered and cold. "I'll do whatever it takes."

Chapter Sixteen

As she drew closer, Elizabeth barely drank in the manicured perfection of the lawns or the scent of the fragrant rosebushes that lined her way. Ivy crept up the sides of the beautiful stone-and-stucco exterior, with some strands even reaching the layered, multicolored roof, and soft light shone out from heavy, leaded-glass windows. There was no time to admire any of this—she had one goal and one goal only.

Shelter.

Elizabeth took a deep breath as she climbed the marble steps to the door. She was going to make this work. Trying to muster a confidence she didn't think she had, she lifted the heavy brass knocker carved in the shape of a lion's head and rapped it twice against the door.

When the door opened, Elizabeth got a peek of

a sumptuous interior. Light streamed out from an opulent chandelier, and the smell of roses was even greater inside than out, courtesy of a huge bouquet that stood on a console table near the door.

"It's about time!" the young woman who stood there said, an anxious expression on her pinched face. Her long, brown hair was pulled back into a lank ponytail, and she wore chinos and a maroon oxford. "You're a little late, aren't you?" she added. "We've been waiting."

Elizabeth swallowed. Who did this girl think she was? She hurriedly tried to think of something to say—something that would prolong her being allowed inside these lovely quarters and not turned back out into the night.

"Deliveries are around the back," the young woman continued. "Straight around." She pointed. "You can't miss it. Your helpers can un-load there."

Unload what? Elizabeth wondered as the girl softly shut the door. She headed in the direction the woman had indicated. At least she hadn't been turned away. Yet.

Elizabeth spotted the delivery entrance almost immediately. The door was partly ajar, and bright light spilled out and onto the surrounding lawns. The most delicious aromas were wafting toward her, making her nostrils twitch and her mouth water. Elizabeth wondered what would happen if they didn't take her on as a dishwasher. What would the penalty be for stealing food? she wondered as her stomach rumbled loudly.

She crept quietly up to the door and peeked timidly around. Best to get the lay of the land before announcing herself.

The delivery entrance was also apparently the kitchen, Elizabeth realized as she peered through the door. The huge, stone-floored room had high mullioned windows; a roaring fire claimed half the wall at one end. A stout older woman in an apron was bustling around, and a beautiful girl with short, raven-colored hair and deep brown eyes who looked to be around Elizabeth's age or maybe a year or two younger was rolling out dough on a marble work island. She too was dressed in chinos and a maroon oxford, which, despite their traditional cut, revealed a body of curves and sinew. The girl who had opened the door for Elizabeth was here as well, removing plates and bowls from a huge dishwasher.

"Vanessa, stop banging that pastry about as if you were beating a rug," the cook admonished the beauty as she whisked by with a huge bowl. Her cockney accent sounded friendly to Elizabeth, especially after the frigidly correct vowels that she'd heard all day.

"What we'll do without Patsy to help out now, I'm sure I don't know," the cook continued, setting down the bowl and eyeing Vanessa with a dubious expression. "She had as light a hand with the pastry as I've ever seen." The cook began stirring whatever was in the bowl.

"Well, *Viscount Maxwell* is not the only one who's allowed to get married, is he?" Vanessa snapped back, wiping her face with the back of her arm, leaving behind a streak of flour. Elizabeth bit her lip at the girl's strong, sarcastic voice. This was the type of girl who could chew you up and spit you out in an instant, making the hair on Elizabeth's neck stand on edge. What she didn't need now was a confrontation. "Patsy's allowed to get married even if she's not *royalty*, you know."

"I agree with Vanessa," said the girl at the dishwasher. Elizabeth noticed as she shot Vanessa a small, timid smile. Vanessa ignored it.

"When *don't* you agree with Vanessa, Alice?" asked the cook, shaking her head.

Who are these people? Elizabeth wondered. They were the kitchen staff, but of what? An inn? An upper-crust English private school?

And *viscount*? Elizabeth wrinkled her brow. What was that? She tried to think if she'd ever come across a viscount in *Pride and Prejudice*, but she was pretty sure that she hadn't. Was that the same thing as an earl? Elizabeth leaned as far as she could around the open door without being seen.

Suddenly the drizzle started up again, and Elizabeth pressed herself against the side of the door, where a short overhang kept her dry.

"Now, you'd best not be letting him hear you call him that," the cook admonished. "You know how Max hates being reminded that he's a member of the peerage."

"Whatever," Vanessa said, shrugging her slim shoulders. For a moment she sounded like she belonged in Sweet Valley more than she did in a fancy London bed-and-breakfast or whatever this place was.

"The fact remains that with Patsy eloping as she has, with no advance warning, we're tremendously short staffed not only for the viscount's wedding, but for the general upkeep of the manor," the cook responded as she poured the contents of the bowl into another bowl.

"Well, if you took on the pastry, I could do more of the prep work for the meals," Vanessa replied. "But we *do* need a scullery maid, and that's a fact. Otherwise we'll be worked to the bone." Her curved crimson lips frowned at the prospect.

"We'll have to advertise," the cook said, walking toward Vanessa. She pinched off a piece of the dough and tasted it. "Needs more rolling," she said, making a face at Vanessa.

Scullery maid? Elizabeth pricked up her ears. She didn't know that scullery maids existed outside of novels by Charles Dickens, but she did know that a job was available, and so was she.

Just then a middle-aged woman, somewhat more formally dressed than the others, walked into the kitchen. Elizabeth ducked back, still watching.

"Are you ready with that tray, Vanessa?" the woman asked as she paused next to a vase of flowers. She began sorting through them, plucking out the blossoms that had started to fade and rearranging the others.

"I'll have it ready in a second, Mary." Vanessa reached for a silver tray and rapidly began layering it with cookies.

"Good," Mary said with a curt nod. She gathered the dead flowers and walked over to the door where Elizabeth was hiding. She quickly tried to dart out of the way, but she wasn't quick enough. Instead of getting out of the way, she found herself staring straight into Mary's ice blue eyes.

"And who might you be?" Mary asked, her eyes narrowed.

Elizabeth straightened her shoulders and smiled with as much confidence as she could muster. "I'm hoping to be your new scullery maid."

Elizabeth sat on a rough wooden stool near the work island, drinking in the warmth of the fire. She was dying for a bowl of the soup that the cook was busy stirring, but she knew that it would be extremely impolite to ask. Instead she concentrated on acting as confident and self-assured as she could, which wasn't easy since she felt like a total impostor.

She looked around her, trying to drink in as many details as possible. The beautiful dark-haired girl—Vanessa—was busy banging dishes around. Was it Elizabeth's imagination, or was she looking at her with scorn? She eyed the dark-haired girl uneasily, but her attention was caught by the crashing of ceramic on stone—Alice had dropped a mug from the dishwasher onto the floor.

"Alice, that's the third time this week!" Mary said impatiently. "One more, and it comes out of your pay. Am I making myself clear?"

"Yes, Mary," replied Alice, flushing.

Poor thing, Elizabeth thought, watching Alice scurry to collect a broom and dustpan and clean up the broken china.

"I'm Mary Dale," the woman said, and Elizabeth snapped to attention. She would have to be on her toes if she was going to pass muster. "I'm the head housekeeper, and I'm in charge of hiring for Pennington House."

Elizabeth nodded at Mary. She wasn't sure what she should say in return. The situation was unlike any she had encountered before. Not only that, but she was hardly at her best. She was so tired and hungry that it was almost impossible for her to think clearly, and she couldn't help being distracted by the aroma of the juicy steaks that the cook had started to prepare.

I can't lose it now, Elizabeth told herself, hoping that her stomach wasn't grumbling too loudly. Now that there was finally light at the end of the tunnel, she was terrified of doing something that would screw things up. She just had to keep it together long enough to pass the interview, and then she could collapse.

"What's your name?" Mary asked.

"Elizabeth—"

She paused. Although it seemed a slim chance, what if she told them her last name and they made a point to find out where she was from? What if they called her family?

"Elizabeth what?" Mary asked, eyeing her.

A terrible feeling of loneliness enveloped her as she realized that she really couldn't give her real name. She was a stranger in a strange land, and if she wanted to stay that way, she'd better rem.... anonymous.

"Bennet," Elizabeth said quickly, the words of *Pride and Prejudice* tumbling together in her jumbled mind. "My name is Elizabeth Bennet."

Vanessa laughed. Mary stared at her. Even the timid Alice was gawking.

Elizabeth prayed that her cheeks wouldn't betray her with a blush. Maybe she'd been too hasty in giving the name of one of England's most famous heroines as her own. Elizabeth blinked at her audience. Maybe she should say that Bennet was her middle name and that her last name was . . . was . . .

She was thinking as fast as she could, but she was suffering from terrible jet lag. She *couldn't* think.

"Elizabeth Bennet!" Vanessa repeated, incredulity on her beautiful face. "Quite a name for an American girl. Are you sure you're not Catherine Earnshaw? Or maybe you're Becky Sharpe?"

Now Elizabeth knew she was blushing as Vanessa hurled the names of two of England's most famous literary characters at her.

Mary Dale quirked an eyebrow at Vanessa. "Vanessa, you'll do well to keep quiet."

With a sniff Vanessa returned to filling the tray with cookies.

"Now, on to more important things," Mary said, turning her attention back to Elizabeth. "Have you done much scullery work before?"

"Of course," Elizabeth said, resisting the urge to cross her fingers behind her back. *Well, I've seen plenty of Merchant-Ivory films, haven't I?* "I'm a good listener and a hard worker. And . . ." She faltered for a moment. "The thing is, I could really use a job."

"Do you have references from your former employers?" Mary asked.

"I've had some bad luck," Elizabeth said, which was true. "My bag with my letters of reference was, uh, stolen at the airport. So I'm afraid I don't," she fibbed. "But the places I worked in are all in America anyway," she added hastily, on the off chance that Mary might decide to ask for phone numbers.

"Hmmm. Well, I daresay, you're probably no worse than most," Mary said as she studied her carefully. Elizabeth had the uncomfortable feeling that she could see right through her. "In any case, I might be able to spare some time to train you," Mary went on thoughtfully. "But that's not the problem."

She's not going to ask for working papers, is she? Elizabeth thought, her heart sinking. She hoped that she hadn't come this close to solving her problems only to be turned away again.

"The problem," Mary continued as she went to check on what Vanessa was doing, "is that we'll need at least a six-month commitment from you." She plucked a rose from one of the large arrangements and placed it in a sterling silver bud vase, which she added to the tray that Vanessa was working on.

Six months? Elizabeth perked up. That didn't sound like a problem to her. That sounded like the best news she'd heard in a long time. She had nowhere else to go. For now and for six months or a year, for that matter.

"That sounds fine," Elizabeth said as neutrally as possible. She didn't want to betray her anxiety by sounding too excited.

"We're rather short staffed at the moment, or I wouldn't be considering you without references in hand," Mary said frankly as she moved throughout the kitchen, checking on things as she went. She had an air of competence that was at once intimidating and reassuring. "One of our maids just left, and Lord Pennington is hosting a rather grand wedding here in six months."

"Lord Pennington?" Elizabeth furrowed her brow. Was she wrong about this being a bed-and-breakfast?

"Yes," Mary said with a nod as she tasted the vinaigrette the cook was making. "A little more chopped shallot, Matilda." Mary turned back to Elizabeth. "This is Pennington House, the residence of the earl of Pennington. His son, Maxwell—Max, as he likes to be called—is getting married in six months, and we have our work cut out for us, preparing for the wedding."

"I see," Elizabeth said, nodding as if she were totally familiar with the ins and outs of British royalty. An earl was a royal, right? Thankfully she hadn't said anything that would have betrayed her ignorance. One thing was clear: Elizabeth obviously wasn't in a bed-and-breakfast. She was in an *earl's* private home.

"The pay isn't much," Mary continued. "Four pounds an hour." She drew a stool up next to Elizabeth and sat down. "But you do get your room and board as well."

Elizabeth's head was whirling. Four pounds an hour was equal to about eight dollars an hour—but more important, her room and board would be paid for as well. An overwhelming surge of emotion came over her, and she fought the impulse to burst into tears. Somehow, some way, in her exhaustion and misery, she had stumbled onto Pennington House, a twist of fate that meant she wasn't going to spend the night huddled on a cold, hard bench, wasn't going to have to show up penniless at the embassy, wouldn't have to go begging like a homeless person for a few pence to buy a cup of tea or piece of bread.

"Do you want the job?" Mary asked bluntly.

"Yes!" Elizabeth blurted out, half afraid Mary would rescind her offer. "Yes, I do." She'd have accepted one pound an hour if it meant she was finally going to get a place to rest.

"Good." Mary nodded. "You'll start tomorrow. Vanessa will show you to your room." Mary waved a hand toward Vanessa, who stared expressionless at Elizabeth. "You'll share a room with Vanessa and Alice, the other two scullery maids here." Mary's expression softened for a second. "I can see that you're nearly asleep on your feet, so you'd best get along to your room and rest up. I'll see you at 7 A.M. sharp to go over your duties."

"Well, come on, Elizabeth *Bennet*," Vanessa said sarcastically.

Elizabeth gathered her duffel bag and her knapsack from where she'd placed them on the floor and followed Vanessa's fast-paced stride out of the kitchen. From Sweet Valley to Chicago to London to Hampstead, the events of the past few weeks, days, hours converged and blurred in Elizabeth's mind. *The nightmare's finally ending,* she thought as she walked quickly up a set of stone steps behind Vanessa.

Elizabeth Bennet was the perfect Austen heroine.

She was smart, she was levelheaded, and she kept her wits about her. If Elizabeth was going to assume a new identity, she couldn't have chosen better, could she?

She knew that she had a lot to deal with in the coming months. It would take a long time to heal, it would take an even longer time than that before she would want to get in touch with her parents again, but she'd crossed the first hurdle. She had a job and a place to stay.

Turn the page for a
sneak peek at
Elizabeth 2:
<u>London</u> <u>Calling</u>.

Chapter One

"And this is the right wing of the first floor of Pennington House, where the earl's office is as well as the main ballroom and library," eighteen-year-old Vanessa Shaw droned, her voice stiff with boredom, her almond-shaped brown eyes dulled and flat, jaded. After all, showing people around Pennington House at the end of a hard day's work was hardly Vanessa's idea of entertainment.

Particularly when that person was the new kitchen maid, Elizabeth Bennet, a girl who already in her short acquaintanceship with Vanessa had proved herself to be a pain in the neck.

"Wow," Elizabeth breathed, panting as she rounded the staircase and entered the ballroom. "What a beautiful wing," she continued reverently, taking in the plush, bloodred carpeting, the oil portraits of the earl of Pennington's lineage lining

2

the walls, the wallpaper threaded through with spun gold, reflecting off the crystal beads of a huge chandelier that hung from the high, vaulted ceiling.

Vanessa flashed Elizabeth a sullen look. The girl was annoying in the extreme, all wide-eyed and impressed and reverent. And then there was the way she looked: so fresh and scrubbed and pearly blond. Everything about Elizabeth screamed earnestness, and Vanessa was not in the mood for earnestness. And she was especially not up for playing tour guide to some young American with title worship.

"What's the family like?" Elizabeth inquired eagerly, her bright blue-green eyes shining with fascination.

Title worship. Vanessa set her small, plump-lipped mouth in a hard line and quickened her pace as she led Elizabeth out of the ballroom and down the long corridor. *Only an American . . . ,* she thought, irked. Only an American could marvel over the myth of the aristocracy, romanticize the royals, breathe reverently at their bloody wallpaper! The whole thing disgusted Vanessa and made her want to slap the curiosity out of Elizabeth's soft face. And a soft face it was. So American girl next door. So sweet and sensitive. Like those girls on that cutesy American series that Alice loved to watch on the telly, *Dawson's Creek.*

3

The kind of clear-eyed perfection Vanessa instinctively loathed.

"What are they like?" Vanessa repeated Elizabeth's question, her mouth twisting into a cold smile of contempt. "They're like all the rest is what they're like!" She blazed down the corridor, enjoying the sounds of Elizabeth struggling to catch up. "The earl is a boor and a bore and has a mouth like a chain saw. Watch yourself or he'll bite your head off!"

Good, Vanessa thought, smiling inwardly at Elizabeth's expression. She'd visibly blanched at Vanessa's words. "And as for his children, Sarah and Max, well, they're absolutely monstrous!"

Excellent! Vanessa couldn't help enjoying Elizabeth's expression. She was like a steadily deflating balloon. "If you don't mind your p's and q's around here," Vanessa continued, stamping on the stairs as she made her way up, "you're toast. Believe me, these people are as soulless as they are spoiled. They're a nightmare to work for, and the atmosphere here is one of complete fear. . . ."

As she gabbed on about Pennington House and its inhabitants, Vanessa threw in a few extra tidbits: The earl hated all the staff and wouldn't lower himself to look you in the eye. If you were ever caught using the main staircase instead of the servants' staircase, you'd be fired without pay. If you were caught standing, the earl would fire you because he's paranoid about eavesdropping . . . *blah blah blah*. . . .

Naturally she was exaggerating. Life in Pennington House was no worse than life in the real world. Vanessa knew that all too well, and she dismissed an unwanted memory of being cold and hungry and being forced to wait in a smoky, smelly bar until her mother finished downing her thirtieth drink of the night. "A quick toot," that's what her mother had always called it. . . .

"I'm not sure I can handle this," Elizabeth murmured, breaking into Vanessa's train of thought as they swept past a giant parlor and down a never-ending passage of studies and libraries. "The family sounds dreadful."

"I see you have good listening skills," Vanessa retorted caustically. "That will come in handy. Because every single day here you get lectured at. Either by Cook or by the housekeeper, Mary Dale. It's a Pennington House tradition. Just like the zipped lip."

"Zipped lip?" Elizabeth looked genuinely worried now as they paused outside the billiard room.

"Zipped lip is key to staying employed as a servant," Vanessa explained, trying to suppress a smile. "If you ever open your mouth and try and defend yourself while being accused of something,

5

you're out on your arse, know what I mean? Speak when spoken *to,* not when spoken *at,* get it?"

"I—I . . . guess so," Elizabeth stammered, her eyes darting nervously from side to side.

"Remember, Elizabeth, you're a scullery maid now," Vanessa hissed as they pressed on and up to the second-floor staircase. "Wherever and whoever you were in Smalltown USA or whatever it's called that you're from, you're just a girl with a sponge and bucket here. Got that?"

Let up a little, Vanessa's inner voice protested as Elizabeth looked more and more crestfallen with each harsh word from Vanessa's mouth. But it was a feeble protest. After all, it was mostly true in spirit if not in fact. There were certainly enough Pennington rules and regs to easily allow Vanessa to monologue away until her seventy-fifth birthday. And okay, so maybe she was spicing them up a bit, highlighting the highlights rather colorfully, but Vanessa felt strongly about her work: which is to say she detested everything about Pennington House and the family who owned it. And she wasn't about to talk them up to some new servant-to-be. Especially when the girl was herself a pest, not to mention a bit of an odd bod.

Elizabeth Bennet. Please. Vanessa had snorted when she'd first heard the Jane Austen heroine's name and seen Elizabeth's pretty and privileged

6

face. Not to mention those hands. ("Yes, I'm familiar with kitchen work. . . .") Vanessa shook her head. The girl had never touched a mop in her life! *What a crock!* All of which only increased her desire to horrify Elizabeth with tales of life as a scullery maid so grim, they'd horrify a Victorian chimney sweep!

"Vanessa?"

At the touch of Elizabeth's cool hand on her arm, Vanessa stopped her fast-paced walk and reluctantly turned. "What is it? We have a lot more ground to cover, you know," she snapped.

"I think I may be in too deep," Elizabeth replied urgently, her eyes clouded with worry. "Really. I think perhaps you're wasting your time giving me the tour. Sounds like I won't last a minute, let alone a day."

Half amused and half annoyed, Vanessa swatted Elizabeth's arm away. "Relax!" she replied with a dry laugh as they passed the earl's sumptuous suite. "You Americans believe everything you hear. Trust me, you *are* actually allowed to breathe here! Tip: Take what I say with a grain of salt. Not a teaspoon," she added gruffly, "a grain."

Marginally relieved, Elizabeth managed a small smile on her still fearful face. Which made Vanessa smile, a secret smirk she didn't want Elizabeth to see. This was exactly where Vanessa wanted her.

Not too terrified, else she'd quit. *And where's the fun in that?*

No, Vanessa didn't want that. For one, they needed another scullery maid, and Vanessa could sure as heck use the extra hands, soft or no. Also, she wanted Elizabeth to stay because it might be mildly entertaining to watch Miss California or wherever she was from make faux pas in front of the fam-damily! Life here was tedious enough, and Vanessa's eyes glinted at the thought of Elizabeth doing something embarrassing, like curtsying to Lady Sarah. . . .

"You'll be fine," Vanessa said coolly as she guided Elizabeth up to the third floor. But she didn't want Elizabeth to get too comfy. *Where's the fun in that either?* No, she would enjoy making Elizabeth do the odd bit of squirming. Like now. "Yes, you'll survive," Vanessa repeated, "but over-all, you'll have a none too easy time here. Might as well be honest about that!"

"Well, okay, but if you think I'll make it through." Elizabeth smiled tentatively. "I mean, if you say so, then maybe I will."

Oh, she was just so coy and sweet, it was nause-ating! "Didn't say that," Vanessa muttered back. Scarily, this girl might be trying to befriend her. And Vanessa did not need a friend. Not here, and sure as hell not now! She had important things to do, and she needed to do those things alone. No use having someone around watching her, snooping on her private time, butting into her business . . .

"On your left, the earl's slob-of-a-son Max's bedroom." Vanessa hurriedly returned to her tour-guide program, fearing that Elizabeth might try to bond with her in some way. "As you can see, it's positively palatial. Bitch to clean too, what with all that leather everywhere. Luckily that's not a part of your job or mine. Kitchen only, for us."

"How long have you been working here?" Elizabeth ventured as Vanessa strode purposefully toward the third-floor servants' staircase, eager to get on with it. *Oh, great, personal-chat time.*

"Six months," Vanessa barked brusquely. *A life sentence,* she thought. "But I'll be out of here soon," she added decisively, lifting her chin. *I damned well will!* Though of course much needed to be done before she could get to that point. She had to—

"Pardon, sorry."

Vanessa turned to see that the speaker in question, twenty-one-year-old Maxwell Pennington, had evidently just wheeled around the balustrade of the main stairwell at top speed and practically knocked Elizabeth off her feet.

"I'm awfully sorry," Max repeated, concern and awkwardness vying for dominance in his face. "Are you all right?"

"Yes, I'm fine. It's okay, really," Elizabeth protested with a sweet smile as Max moved to steady her with a hand at her elbow.

"I'm afraid it's my penchant for Häagen-Dazs," Max explained sheepishly. "When I get my after-dinner cravings for cherry chocolate, I just bullet down the stairs, and woe betide anyone who gets in my way! Awfully rude really, sorry."

He laughed a little, nervously. So did Elizabeth.

Vanessa rolled her eyes. It didn't take a brain surgeon to figure out that there was some chemistry happening here. From the nervous, rather idiotic smile on Max's chiseled face to the way his dark eyes darted up and down, drinking in Elizabeth from head to toe, he was clearly quite taken with her. And as for Elizabeth, well, her flushed cheeks combined with the embarrassed yet at the same time curious look in her eyes was a dead giveaway. *We have a love connection,* Vanessa thought. *How charming.*

And how utterly unrealistic!

"Who was that?" Elizabeth whispered as Max traipsed down to the kitchen.

"You haven't figured it out?" Vanessa was incredulous. "You're not half bright then, are you, Lizzie? It's Max Pennington. Son of the earl. The future Lord Pennington himself."

"He seems much nicer than I expected,"

10

Elizabeth remarked as the girls took the final flight of stairs to the fourth floor.

"That's just an act," Vanessa explained. Not that Vanessa had any proof of that. But then again, she'd only been here six months. He still had time to show his true Pennington colors, and Vanessa did not doubt that he would.

"An act? Really?" Skepticism flickered across Elizabeth's features.

Only three seconds of meeting and already she wants to defend him! Vanessa wrinkled her nose in disgust as they made their way down the corridor. "Do yourself a favor, Elizabeth," she warned acidly. "Forget Max. For one, he's what I believe in your country is known as a jerk. I'm afraid they're born that way. For two, he's engaged to be married in six months' time to Lavinia, the duchess of Louster, and trust me, you do not want to cross paths with her. It's their royal wedding we'll be slaving over for the next six months, by the way."

"But he looks so young," Elizabeth replied doubtfully.

"Twenty-one," Vanessa confirmed as they arrived at a small wooden door. "Old enough to get hitched to the witch. Who is herself only nineteen. A child bride by modern standards. Practically on the shelf by British noble tradition." Vanessa took

11

a key from her pocket. "The duchess," she continued, "is, shall we say, a chip off the old ice block. Her father, the earl of Louster—thankfully dead—was a dreadful man and Lord Pennington's best friend. The duke of Louster was feared by all, despised by anyone brave enough to have an opinion. . . ."

Tone it down, Vanessa's inner voice suggested as she continued to enumerate just how hideous Lavinia and her father were. But Vanessa ignored her better instincts. Watching Elizabeth suck it all up and quake in her Reebok sneakers was simply too delicious to pass up. And was this girl ever impressionable!

". . . So I'd stay far from Lavinia if you're at all allergic to snake bites," Vanessa concluded as they entered the bedroom. "And this is our plush suite," she intoned sarcastically. "Bathroom in corner, your bed and closet are to the far left. We share with Alice Henry, who is mostly Mary's help but ours too. Alice is dull as a block of cement and has the IQ of a crustacean, but she minds herself, stays out of the way. Here's your key," Vanessa added, shoving her hand into her pocket and tossing Elizabeth a gold Yale on a rusty ring.

Elizabeth caught it. "Thanks." She looked warily around her and then mustered what Vanessa could see was a brave smile rather than a genuine one. "And thanks for showing me around. And for warning me about witchy Lavinia," Elizabeth joked feebly.

Somehow this annoyed Vanessa. Was Elizabeth going to continue to attempt to chum up to her?

"It's not a joke," Vanessa retorted coldly, "unless you find unemployment funny. Lavinia will have you out on your bum in no time if you don't take her seriously, Elizabeth. And that goes for the rest of these people." She leveled her cold eyes at Elizabeth, who was by this time sitting on her bed, looking somewhat hunched and anxious. "You think Lavinia sounds bad?" Vanessa continued nastily. "Well, she is an angel of mercy compared with Sarah, the earl's spitfire of a daughter. You stay out of her way," she added, "and while you're about it, stay out of mine too!"

With that, Vanessa turned and made for the door. As she turned, she couldn't help the tweak of sympathy that snaked through her insides. Elizabeth really looked the worse for wear. Worn out. Dark circles. Alone. Vanessa knew that feeling only too well.

Too bad, she thought as she turned the brass doorknob, stepped out, and jerked the door shut, hardening herself against any impulse to pop off a kind word to help Elizabeth deal with her first night in the house. But Vanessa wasn't exactly the kind-word type, the warm-welcome type.

She was more of the tough-cookie type.

Yet another thing this Elizabeth Bennet had better learn and learn fast . . . if she knows what's good for her!

What have you gotten yourself into, Elizabeth Wakefield?

Bennet! Elizabeth corrected herself. *It's Elizabeth Bennet now. Elizabeth Wakefield is out of the picture! You didn't want to give your real last name, and you'll have to remember that!*

Her eyes moistened with tears, tears that had been threatening to arrive for over forty-eight hours. Tears she'd managed to swallow back. Until now.

It had all been too much, and Vanessa's chilly presence was the last straw. And so after an evening spent walking miles through her formidably massive new home, Elizabeth lay back on her bed and let the hot salt water run down her cheeks and seep into her hair. Choking back a loud sob, she tried to get ahold of herself, tried to lie still and take deep breaths, but the single cot was somewhat unforgiving. Especially compared with the double futon with extra padding she was used to at home . . .

Home! A feeling of longing washed over her, and Elizabeth's eyes burned. She was absolutely

14

exhausted. She was jet-lagged from the flight to London she'd taken a day earlier and emotionally ravaged by everything that had happened. . . .

Home. Suddenly the word seemed less appealing and luckily far, far away and at least a year ago. Was it really only two days since she'd had such a blowout with her parents in the Chicago airport? Really only two days since she'd hopped a plane for England bound for her semester abroad on scholarship at the University of London, only to find that she hadn't responded by the deadline and that her place had been given to another student?

Elizabeth half sniffed, half sobbed at the thought of that disappointment. And there was no one to turn to either. For the first time in her life Elizabeth couldn't simply pick up the phone and call a friend, much less a family member. She'd never felt this alone. Totally penniless, she'd ended up riding the tube to her last hope, a youth hostel where she'd hoped to hook up with a friend she'd made in Illinois. Pennington House had shone in the distance, and she'd headed over, praying they'd let her spend the night for free. She'd ended up with a job as a kitchen maid, with room and board in addition to a small salary.

But you're lucky, Elizabeth reminded herself as she pushed a tangle of tear-soaked blond hair from her cheek. It was true. The job as kitchen maid was, though unglamorous and hardly what she'd come to England for, nevertheless a lifesaver.

And Elizabeth needed to make it work. It was either that or accept defeat and go home to Sweet Valley. Home to her family. Home to Jessica, who'd forced her to run away in the first place.

At the thought of Jessica a fresh swell of tears rose up through the back of Elizabeth's throat. Finding Jessica, her twin, her best friend, all over Sam Burgess. *My boyfriend!* And they were clearly about to have sex! It had been a total moment of shock for Elizabeth. For one, Sam and Jessica had always hated each other. Yet now they were both prepared to betray Elizabeth for each other?

It was awful. It was ludicrous. It was . . . *over*. Elizabeth shuddered, then forced her mind away from the things that were hurting her. She needed to take a bath and get a good night's sleep. And she needed to keep her thoughts from wandering down paths that only gave her pain.

Think about the positive, she ordered herself, swinging her legs off the bed and ignoring the wave of jet lag that demanded she lie down and sleep for a month. *You're here, and you're Elizabeth Bennet.* And though of course neither of those two things was the most amazing thing to be just now, Elizabeth knew the other options were worse. *After all, who would want to be Elizabeth Wakefield?*

16

Elizabeth asked herself, making herself stand up. *It's not as if that girl had anything going for her!*

Elizabeth winced, but though it hurt, the truth was the truth. Elizabeth Wakefield did indeed have nothing left. Because everything she'd thought she'd had was destroyed in one single moment . . .

Enough of that! Elizabeth walked over to her suitcase, unzipped it briskly, and got busy. Unpacking would take her mind off things. It was exactly what she needed. As was this house and this job. No matter how awful, this was a fresh start.

Still. Elizabeth worried as she hung up a sundress. Caustic Vanessa had managed to get under her skin. For someone as pretty and pixielike as Vanessa, it was a shock to see what a sharp tongue she had. Sure, it was obvious the girl was just trying to scare her, but there had to be at least some truth to all the things she was saying. Elizabeth swallowed. No question about it, she had good reason to be fearful. Pennington House, whose elaborate hierarchy and code of etiquette was as confusing as its floor plan. It was enough to make her brain swirl into total fuzz.

Elizabeth sat down on her bed again and looked out the window onto the manicured lawns that rolled off into the distance, illuminated a silvery gray by a thick band of moonlight. The place was impressive, all right, but also totally formidable.

Earls, dukes, duchesses, lords, ladies, maids, maids-in-waiting, house cleaners, housekeepers . . . the nuances and differences were so numerous as to be completely overwhelming, and she felt a headache pinching at her temples. *What kind of world is this?* Certainly not a world she knew, this world of polo clubs and servants' staircases and arranged marriages and people with complicated titles . . .

At that, Max Pennington's handsome face swam into Elizabeth's thoughts. He'd seemed pretty down-to-earth, though. With his Calvin Klein jeans, red polo shirt, bare feet, and sheepish grin, he certainly didn't seem like someone Elizabeth ought to fear. In fact, he'd seemed like just another very cute, very charming guy. A six-foot-two, square-jawed handsome kind of guy. The kind of guy she wouldn't mind getting to know.

In another world! Elizabeth admonished herself, shooting to her feet and returning to her unpacking. *Here, he's a sir to you!*

As she placed her one pair of heeled sandals into the back of her closet, Elizabeth forced herself to stick to the facts of her situation. Like Max being out of reach and the pretty shoes: completely useless now. This was a new world with new obligations and new rules. But that didn't mean she had to hate it. After all, the room could have been much worse. Yes, it was fairly spartan, but it was also kind of cozy, and the girls had their own very large, deep, freestanding claw-footed bathtub. Things like that were big pluses in a week of almost total minuses.

And if she didn't like it, Elizabeth knew she had only to revisit her botched attempts to make a life for herself in London. *So much for that!* Elizabeth zipped up her empty suitcase and stashed it behind her closet, her jaw clenched in determination as she dismissed a last, fading image of herself busily attending seminars and fiction workshops at the University of London, sipping Twinings English breakfast tea with friends and discussing contemporary British fiction.

But it was time to give up pipe dreams, time to get with the program.

Elizabeth Bennet, scullery maid. This was her life now.